# NOW WITH FLEAS!

# MARGARET STOHL
### AND LEWIS PETERSON

# CATS VS. ROBOTS 2

# NOW WITH FLEAS!

## ILLUSTRATED BY KAY PETERSON

KT KATHERINE TEGEN BOOKS
*An Imprint of HarperCollins Publishers*

Katherine Tegen Books is an imprint of HarperCollins Publishers.

Cats vs. Robots #2: Now with Fleas!
Copyright © 2019 by Margaret Stohl and Lewis Peterson

Library of Congress Cataloging-in-Publication Number: 2019944618
ISBN 978-0-06-266573-7

Typography by Andrea Vandergrift
19 20 21 22 23   PCL/LSCH   10 9 8 7 6 5 4 3 2 1
❖
First Edition

This book is dedicated to all the
young people
who
speak up
and
take action
to make the world
safer, cleaner, more tolerant, and fair.
Thanks for Being the Flea.
This book is also dedicated to Charlie
with thanks
for coming up with all the good ideas
as usual
and even the title.
—M, L & K

# THE KNOWN GALAXY

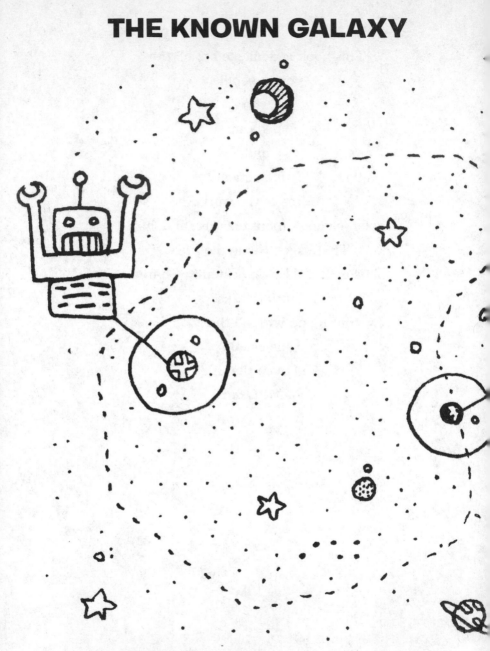

## LEGEND

**PLANET BINAR,** home world of the Binars (metal-heads), HQ of the Galactic Robot Federation

 **PLANET FELINUS,** home world of the Cats (four-leggers), HQ of the Great Feline Empire

**PLANET EARTH,** home world of Humans (Furless/two-leggers), HQ of nothing in particular

# 1

## Huggs Held Back

As it turns out, you can be very, very rich and still feel very, very small.

Very, very powerful, and still feel very, very powerless.

Case in point: bosses.

Really, most bosses of most companies everywhere, but in particular, this boss, of this one, right here.

Because here in the vast, cavernous darkness of the futuristic headquarters of GloboTech Incorporated, an angry-looking boss of a man sat and stared at a wall . . .

. . . feeling small.

The longer he stared at the wall, which was also a screen, the angrier he became and the smaller he felt.

It wasn't the wall that was the problem. (Of course not; the custom fifty-foot enhanced-ultra-extreme-definition-flat-screen wall was his favorite thing in the world, at least most days.)

It was the *contents* of the screen wall that triggered the boss man.

Every inch of it, every millimeter, was crammed edge to edge with information—images and videos, charts and figures, gifs and memes and streams, all flashing and updating in dizzying, constant motion.

The boss man's bloodshot eyes fixated on one part of the collage, a large blue rectangle filled with tiny white words that scrolled and flowed downward like a digital waterfall.

At least, that's what he was *expecting* to see.

At the moment, the only thing in the blue rectangle was a glowing red window blinking ALL CAPS warning messages like "HOUSE SYSTEM FAILURE!" and "NETWORK ACCESS DENIED!"

The turtlenecked man's unusually long fingers, carefully steepled beneath his too-large-for-his-face nose and his bald speckled quail egg of a head, began to quiver.

He was a tensed spring, ready to snap. A bottle rocket about to blast off. A rattrap about to—

*BRRRAAP!*

The immaculately manicured pug perched in the boss man's lap lifted his head and busted out a breathtaking booty bomb. A poopy puff of pug perfume. A real fur-filtered nose nuke of a . . .

Well, a classic puppy fart.

The blast echoed off the high ceiling, and the man rubbed his tired eyes, muttering to himself with irritation.

"Failure. Denied. Failure. Denied." His mutterings grew louder. "FAILURE?! DENIED?!" He was shouting at the screen now. "WHAT IS THIS GARBAGE?!"

Startled, the pungent pug slipped down from the man's lap and retreated quietly behind the desk.

Failure was not a word this particular fellow was used to—

"FAIL? I DON'T FAIL!" the man shrieked at nobody.

Because the fellow in question was—

"DON'T YOU KNOW WHO I AM?!"

The fellow was—

"I AM THE ONE AND ONLY GIFFORD MICHAEL EDWARD HUGGS!!!"

Indeed.

The frustrated man was none other than Gifford "Giff" M.E. Huggs, the world-famous CEO of GloboTech and, not to mention—as he would always mention—

"I AM THE RICHEST PERSON IN THE WORLD!!!"

There it is.

Giff M.E. Huggs did not—

*"I DO NOT—"*

He never—

*"EVER—"*

Failed.

*"GIFF M.E. HUGGS DOES NOT FAIL!"*

Huggs growl-shouted again. He swept an important-looking stack of confidential papers and files off his desk. Post-it Notes exploded into the air like confetti.

Huggs began to speed-pace around the room.

His spindly arms swung wide, and his small, well-trained feet never left the ground—in keeping with the flawless form and discipline he had perfected through years of competitive speed-walking. Speed-pacing, his team of GloboTech in-house therapists said, was a healthy way to calm anger issues. At least, healthier than his previous methods of speed-window-breaking, speed-fire-setting, and speed-Ferrari-crashing.

But this raging Huggs was a side the mogul didn't often show. To the world, he was known as the wise and friendly neighborhood billionaire; the composed, dignified, ultra-wealthy—if egg-headed and oddly proportioned—man who had it all.

And truthfully, by many standards—or, by money standards—he did. Huggs had more bank than the average bank, even the average country, and he prided himself on that.

His infatuation with accumulation began with a gift from his miserly grandfather and guardian, Gavin "Gave" Newman Olson Huggs. It was the only gift little Giff ever received from his grandfather, and was his most prized possession: a porcelain Puggy Bank.

Gave N.O. Huggs was a stingy coot, spare with money as well as love, but the young Giff M.E. Huggs idolized him. Desperate for his approval, little Giff was driven, obsessed even, by an unrelenting need to fill that Puggy Bank over and over.

*Is it full enough now, Grandpa?*

Poor little Giff asked this question more times than he could count, and *every* time, Gave N.O. Huggs would squint over his square spectacles, mouth turned downward in a permanent frown, and shake his head.

"Almost," he would say, and turn back to his work.

Grandpa Huggs was long gone, but the younger Huggs never stopped trying to fill that bank.

He had more money than he could possibly spend, although he did his best to try. He bought enormous mansions, small islands, large islands, yachts that could hover and survive any natural disaster, parking garages full of cars (*self-driving, self-flying, self-floating*), and his own copy of the Declaration of Independence.

He even bought the vice president of the United States, Parker P. Pants, although owning VP P.P. Pants was the one thing he could not openly brag about. Not that it made it any less true.

Indeed, most people couldn't imagine having a fortune so enormous, but Giff M.E. Huggs knew he could always have more. His grandfather's cold disapproval was on permanent autoplay in his mind, drilling an unfillable hole in his soul.

*"Almost,"* he heard when he counted his cash. To Huggs, the word *almost* was worse than any four-letter word you could imagine (and please don't try).

For example, if he had children, and they rushed home excited about getting a near-perfect score on the hardest math test imaginable, best in the school, he would *almost* be proud of them.

Those poor children would *almost* be allowed to eat dinner rather than spend the rest of the night correcting their one mistake, over and over.

So yes, Giff M.E. Huggs got *a little* upset when he wanted something and couldn't have it. Especially when he *almost* had his hands on it.

Like now.

Huggs speed-paced back to his desk, focused on only one thing.

*Bratty children.*

The thing that got in his way.

*Annoying twins.*

The ones who had *almost*-ed him.

*Nobody gets the better of me.*

Huggs tapped an invisible touch pad on the surface of his desk and zoomed in on a blurry picture of a family, a mother, father, and twin children.

He zoomed closer on the twins, fingers trembling.

*Especially not them.*

If it weren't for those two, he would be busy planning his next acquisition, not hiding in a dark room, speed-pacing, licking his wounds.

*Max and Min Wengrod.*

*Horrible children, with horrible parents that almost surely spoil them.*

He growled and tapped again, bringing up a satellite image of a small, shabby home in Los Angeles. In the poorly maintained front yard (so overgrown it was obvious even from orbit, Huggs noted with disdain), he saw the outlines of two small spaceships parked on the lawn.

"There they are. . . . Look at that." Huggs leaned forward. "Are you looking at this?"

"I'm looking at it," a disembodied voice echoed out

from a speaker imbedded in the wall. "I was also there," the voice added, sounding a little bitter. "If you recall."

The voice, belonging to an AI program named House was, indeed, a little bitter. GloboTech had been using House as a corporate spy in the Wengrod house, until its cover was blown and the Wengrods got the better of it.

"I do recall," Huggs said through clenched teeth, "how you fumbled everything, right at the finish line. When we were SO CLOSE!"

The voice went silent.

Huggs tapped at the touch pad. Through hazy black-and-green night vision, he watched small, odd-sized shapes shuttle between the house and the ships, some on four legs, some on one.

Suddenly, an intense flash flooded the scene—reflecting off that shiny eggshell Huggs called a head—and only one ship remained, cat-shaped.

Huggs tapped again and pulled up a cluster of satellite images showing the curved surface of Earth, dark and cloud-covered. A second flash of light lit the clouds below.

The camera centered on the flash and refocused on the ship as it burst through the clouds, escaping Earth's atmosphere at impossible speeds, leaving a quickly fading trace of billowing smoke.

The sight of the ship leaving orbit triggered a new

level of Huggs rage. He shouted toward his wall speakers.

"HOW COULD YOU LET THEM GET AWAY?"

Huggs kicked away from the desk, knocking it over with a thundering crash.

*PFFPPLPLLPT!*

The pug yelped and farted—er, yarted—scrambling to a safer distance on stubby legs.

"How did this go so wrong, House?" Huggs resumed speed-pacing, trying to regain some composure. He went through his routine. *Heel-toe. Heel-toe. Breathe out the heat. Breathe in the sweet. . . .*

"Is that a rhetorical question, sir?"

"It's a *question* question, House." *Heel-toe. Heel-toe. Breathe out the pain. Breathe in the gain. . . .*

"Actually, I would argue that many things went quite right," House sniffed. "Granted, we did not capture the Singularity Chip, or the plans to create one, and true, both ships were able to leave Earth. . . ."

"But, House—" Huggs sucked down his rage, hopping in place like a poorly proportioned frog. "Were those . . . were they not . . . in fact . . . THE ONLY THINGS THAT MATTERED?!"

The twins Max and Min Wengrod—not to mention Max's kittens and Min's robots—had managed to keep House, Huggs, and GloboTech from taking control of the Singularity Chip invented by the Wengrod parents. The

Singularity Chip was one of a kind—worth more than all other technology in the solar system, combined.

Huggs wanted the chip.

"If I may," House said, taking control of the screen. The view zoomed back to a close-up of the surveillance video of the house.

Huggs pinched the bridge of his nose, flopping back down into his chair. "Go on."

House cycled through images of the Wengrod property. "I suggest we focus on what we learned and use that to move forward. By going back. Return to the scene of the crime. Ground zero, the Wengrod home. We need eyes on the creators if we want the chip."

Huggs stared. "You're right. We need to know what's going on. We need you to get back into that house. With the . . . Snodgrods? Hogdogs? Wengrods?"

House crackled. "Unfortunately, it can't be me this time. The Wengrods . . . er, deleted me. I've been erased from their systems entirely. Utterly firewalled."

"So you're useless?" Huggs raised an eyebrow.

"Temporarily." House sounded defeated.

"Fine." Huggs eyed the video feed. "We'll use the Roachbot."

"The top secret surveillance robot you're developing for the CIA?" House pulled up a series of classified GloboTech schedules and blueprints. "It appears the prototype is still weeks from being completed."

"Come up with a better idea, House. Until then, seeing as you've been . . . evicted, this is the best plan for infiltrating that shabby shack."

The speakers crackled again. "Affirmative."

As the AI logged out, the walls switched back to an image of the cat ship leaving the solar system.

Huggs reached down into the shadows and picked up his small, stinky companion. He scratched the pug's chin folds as he stared at the stars on the screen in front of him, considering his options:

. . . *get control of that chip* . . .

. . . *fill a galaxy-sized Puggy Bank, while you're at it* . . .

. . . *and show those snotty kids they don't want to mess with Huggs* . . .

The pug gave Huggs's cheek a lick and squeaked out the tiniest toot.

.

.

.

*PFFFFFFFT!*

# 2

# Watching Wengrods (weeks later)

Just as you can't judge a book by its cover, or a boss by their Puggy Bank, you also can't judge a family by how recently they've mowed their lawn or painted their house.

This was the case, at least, for the family who lived in the two-story red-tiled hacienda on Bayside Road, known to the locals as "the Wengrods."

The Los Angeles summer sun cast a yellowish glow on the peeling paint and weathered exterior of the Wengrods, but inside, the home was anything but shabby.

It was clean, sleek, modern, and (for now) quiet, as a host of smart devices around the house hummed silently along, doing their smart things. Laundry was washed and folded. Dishes cleaned and sorted. Dust dutifully swept up and discarded.

In contrast, two kittens on the couch splayed and stretched lazily, asleep. Stu and Scout were also smart—as in *smart-mouthed*—but the only thing they were diligent about was eating and sleeping.

In the guest bathroom nearby, a toilet gurgled. Stu's ear twitched at the sound. It was one of his favorite sounds of all, right up there with the shaking-snack-bin sound, the kibble-hitting-bowl sound, and the fridge-opening sound. But today he was too deep into his nap to go investigate, and the sound went otherwise unnoticed.

*BLOOP!*

The water in the toilet rippled and an oily, brackish bubble rose to the water's surface . . . and popped.

Then another . . . and another . . .

*PLUP! BLUP! PLUP!*

Along with the bubbles, dark clouds rose from the bottom of the water, reaching slowly toward the surface. . . .

*PLOOOOP!*

A disgusting lump of foul-smelling goo rose to the water's surface—no, not *that* goo—

**13**

—and out of it a small mechanical cockroach emerged, legs churning, antennae searching. A microscopic logo on its thorax was stamped with the logo for GloboTech.

In a flash, the robotic roach crawled out of the water. It scaled up the sides of the toilet bowl, dropped to the floor, and zigzagged into the shadows, hiding itself in the dark corner crack between the bathroom wall and the bathroom cabinet.

*BRRRPBRRRPBRRRPBRRRP!*

It emitted a series of ultrasonic pulses, vibrating until it was clean—and the corner was decidedly not.

The GloboTech Roachbot had arrived.

Two tiny red sensors glowed as the Roachbot consulted an internal map of its surrounding environment . . . found its bearings . . . and shot out and under the inch-high gap beneath the bathroom door, heading for the living room.

The Roachbot scurried from shadow to shadow, antennae twitching as it searched for the optimal location. This home was, as the CIA would say, a target-rich environment, but Roachbot knew what it needed.

There, on the bookshelf.

Roachbot detected the internet-connected pet cam that Max used to check on Stu and Scout during the day. Shelf by shelf, it scurried and crawled, and eventually settled on top of the camera.

Microprobes extended from its mouth, through joints in the internet-connected camera, and in moments, Roachbot had hacked into the camera, ready to broadcast the sights and sounds of the Wengrod home back to GloboTech.

Then the show began.

\* ⋈ \*

The front door slammed open as Max Wengrod followed his twin sister, Min, into the front hall. As always, the twins' return was followed by two familiar sounds:

*DUHM-DUHM.*

The first sound, right on schedule, came from kitten paws as they gently hit the floor. *That's Scout,* Max thought happily.

*THUMP-THUMP.*

Next came the sound of a less graceful landing. *And Stu.* Max grinned. Stu seemed to be enjoying domestic life and had put on quite a belly since moving into a home with regular mealtimes.

Max dropped his backpack to the floor and flopped down, exhausted. "These days are just too long."

*BADUMP BADUMP BADUMP!*

The two kittens scampered around the corner. They were always happy to see the Wengrod twins, especially

Max, who had saved them weeks ago from being washed away down the LA River.

The smaller kitten—a long, spotted pink-nosed cat, roughly the shape of a string bean—crept closer, greeting Max by affectionately chewing on his hair.

"Scout, not now," Max said, gently pushing her away. "And what did we say about eating hair? It's gross."

"Especially if you knew the last time he showered," Min said, making a face. She bent to hold out her hand, wiggling her fingers until Scout trotted over.

Though Min had only recently discovered her love for any pets, other than the robots she built with her father, she had been making up for lost time, and had come to love the kittens as much as Max did.

"Stu, where are ya, bud?" Max hollered from the floor, waving his hand above his head and waiting for kitten teeth to find it. Instead, he felt the familiar and friendly headbutt in his side.

Max sat up to see Scout's sturdier brother, Stu, hunting for affection. He scratched Stu behind the ears. "Ah, you missed me, didn't you, buddy?"

*PURRRRRRRR.*

The growling coming from Stu's chest was all the answer Max needed.

"Of course they did. We've been gone almost as

long as a regular school day." Min sighed. "And I'm starving. We need snacks."

Max and the kittens followed Min into the kitchen. There, as usual, a small army of domestic robot prototypes—built by Min and her father and known as the Protos—were getting Max and Min's after-school snack ready.

The sight of battered old Joan Drone, with one broken propeller, hovering by the cupboard with a bag of chips—or of Drags the treaded tank, trailing laundry behind him as he rolled from the laundry room into the kitchen, waving two clean cloth napkins straight from the dryer—or of Cy, the cyclone spinner, waving packs of fruit snacks excitedly over his head—or of Tipsy, the semi-successful self-balancing robot, who was facedown on the floor trying to see what she could see when she could see nothing at all—well, all those things might have looked odd to another brother and sister, but in the Wengrod house, they just looked like home.

"Thanks, Joan," Min said, taking a bag of her favorite dill-pickle-flavored chips from Joan's grasper, and sliding into a seat at the kitchen table.

Joan bobbled and whirred away, heading over to Max.

Max took his chips and sank into the chair next to Min. "A summer camp about games sounded awesome,

**17**

but I just want to *play* games now, not learn how to make them."

"I mean," Min said, accepting her fruit snacks from Tipsy, "obviously I want to be an astronaut, and yes, I really wanted to work at NASA during the summer, but why didn't someone warn me that it would be so much, you know, *work*?"

"Tell me about it." Max ripped open his pack, sending fruit snacks flying. "Meanwhile, it's not like Obi and the whole fate of the universe isn't depending on us."

Max and Min were the only two kids on Earth—the *Furless* planet, as the Felines called it—who knew about the intergalactic war between the Felines of the Great Feline Empire and the Binars of the Robot Federation.

Cats vs. Robots.

Making things worse, while Max and Min were home eating chips and tickling kittens, someone they loved was far away and in trouble, and it was up them to bring him home.

*Obi.*

A few weeks had passed since the tense standoff between House from GloboTech, Pounce from the Great Feline Empire, and Beeps from the Robot Federation. The conflict was over the Wengrod parents' invention, the Singularity Chip, and an old cat named Obi from next door.

That was the night Max and Min's parents miraculously saved Obi, in more ways than one—first by making a copy of his mind and memories, then by transferring them into the Singularity Chip and a brand-new cat-like robot body, just as Obi reached the end of his ninth and final life.

It had seemed like a happy ending, until Beeps showed up and cat-napped Robo-Obi, stealing him away to Binar.

Nobody had heard a word from either Beeps or Obi since.

Pounce left to get help from the Felines, promising to contact Max and Min as soon as he got back to Felinus.

Nobody had heard from Pounce since that night either.

\* ⌖ \*

"You're back!" Cousin Javi came in and sat down across from Max and Min, placing an environmental law textbook and a precariously balanced stack of folders and papers on the table in front of them. ("Them," not "him" or "her," because Javi was nonbinary and used "they"/"them" as pronouns.)

Javi was working for an environmental law nonprofit during summer break from studying law. The project, as it just so happened, was suing the richest man on earth, Gifford M.E. Huggs, who wanted to keep people from using a dirt path that cut through the side yard of his massive oceanfront Malibu mansion to get to a public beach.

"Hey, Javi," Min said.

"Mumph-mumph," Max said, swallowing the last of the fruit snacks.

"Why the long faces?" Javi poked Max in the shoulder.

"It's Obi. We still don't have a plan to rescue him. We don't even know if he's okay," Max said glumly.

Stu sat on Max's foot, offering what comfort he could.

Scout, always on the prowl, jumped up on the table to investigate the new smells. A new person in the room, a new stack of papers, a new book. Scout even caught a glorious whiff of backpack, the mother of all smell buffets, though it wasn't in sight.

But the first, the teetering stack of papers. Something that knock-down-able was just too tempting to pass up, by kitten logic.

Scout paused to sniff the stack, then stretched up for a better look, reaching out with her paw to give it just the *smallest* . . .

*little* . . .

*nudge.* . . .

*BOOP!*

"No!" Javi said, too late, as the pile toppled over.

"Scout!" Min yelled. Scout scrabbled off the table and streaked out of the room as the papers flew into the air.

"It's okay," Javi said with a sigh. "Sounds like we all got more than we bargained for this summer. I feel guilty too. I've been so busy with my internship I haven't had much time to focus on how to get Obi back from those robots myself."

*WHRRRRRRR.*

Joan Drone hovered behind Javi, with a waiting Capri Sun. Javi took it. "Thanks, Joan. You always know what to . . . say."

Max pulled a golden medallion shaped like a pyramid out of his pocket. It dangled from a small braided collar, just like the one Obi wore. He placed it on the table in front of them.

"Is that Obi's communicator? The one he wore on his collar?" Javi asked.

Max shook his head. "Pounce gave me this one. It's the same as Obi's—it's how the two of them communicated, for all those years."

Min looked at her brother. "And? Have you heard anything from Pounce?"

Max shook his head sadly, tapping on it for the

millionth time. He even tried holding it up to his mouth, like it was a microphone. "Hello? Pounce? Can anybody hear me?"

Min pulled it away. "Come on, Max. You know that thing only works if Pounce calls first."

"It does?" Javi looked surprised.

"The medallion was designed for Great Feline Empire explorers who operated in secret. Only some-one on the home planet can start communication," Min explained.

"Tricky," Javi said.

"Or annoying." Max snorted. "Like a broken space phone with no buttons."

Min looked at him. "Pounce said he would contact us when he could. We just have to be patient." She was losing patience herself.

Min couldn't help but worry about the old cat. "And not just because he's an awesome robo-cat now," she always felt compelled to say, though she knew everyone still thought of Max as the cat lover and Min as the cat hater—Max as the flaky artist and Min as the sensible roboticist—Max as the slacker gamer and Min as the straight-A programmer.

*Well, at least that part is true.*

It was also true that Min was highly allergic to cats,

but she had learned to wash her hands after petting Stu and Scout, to not touch her eyes, and to keep the door to her bedroom shut. She adapted to the kittens because they made Max so happy, and they were part of her family now. *And, okay, they're kinda cute too.*

Min had also learned that even when a person changed how they felt about something, the world didn't necessarily change with them. Everyone still thought of her as the cat hater, even though it wasn't true and made her feel sort of bad.

She heard the sound of a snore and looked down to where Stu was napping under the table, Max's shoelace in his mouth. Scout had snuck back in and was curled up next to him, thumping her tail nervously as she kept her eyes on, well, anything that moved.

Min smiled, suddenly feeling hopeful.

*If someone like me can like both cats and robots once I really know them, maybe anyone can? And maybe that means a cat-like robot stuck on a robot planet will be okay. Or a robot-cat war will . . . end . . . okay?*

She wasn't sure, but she was determined not to give up. "We'll hear from Pounce soon," she said. "He seemed very . . . responsible."

"Especially for a cat," Javi agreed. "I mean, he did organize the pen drawer, and he doesn't even have fingers."

"I just wish I knew what Obi was doing." Max sighed. "He must be so scared."

And so the three Wengrods waited, staring at the alien collar communicator, worrying over the fate of a mechanical cat on a faraway planet, and wishing he would just call home.

# 3

# A Raging Robot

**T**HWACKKK!

Across the galaxy, on the faraway planet Binar, the heavy doors to the Royal Elevator slammed shut. The gleaming chrome rectangle jolted and launched upward with a shake and a groan.

*KLANG!*

The rough launch sent Sir Beeps-a-Lot backward, and he crashed into a reflective wall. "Gah! This elevator needs maintenance!"

The other passenger said nothing.

Beeps straightened his bent antennae and began

compulsively rolling back and forth on his solitary wheel, the Binar version of anxious pacing.

The other passenger was the robotic feline creature formerly known as Obi, or as the Protos called him, OB_1_Catno_B. He sat calmly on the reflective elevator floor staring at Beeps, wondering if now his name should be OB_2_Catno_B. . . .

"What are you looking at?" Beeps grouched.

Obi opened and closed his mouth, saying nothing. His mind, however, was whirling.

<< This place is Binar, home of the Robot Federation. >>

<< That entity is Beeps, a Federation Robot. >>

<< I am Obi, a Cat from the Furless planet. >>

<< But I am also Obi, a Robot from the Wengrod lab. >>

<< Thus, at present, I cannot be said to be wholly Cat or wholly Robot . . . or wholly Obi . . . >>

<< And while I know I am not Home, not with my Boy . . . >>

<< . . . I am uncertain if a not-Cat-not-Robot-not-Obi can reasonably expect to have a Home or a Boy at all. >>

The thought filled Obi with sadness. He found himself automatically activating the neural sensors that raised one paw to his face, as if to brush a tear from the place where they used to flow and catch upon his whiskers.

That was not the case now.

*BWOOOOONG!*

Beeps rammed into the side of the elevator again but couldn't blame the elevator this time.

Obi lowered his metal paw. "You are nervous."

"Why would I be nervous? Because I'm going to have to introduce a . . . you . . . to the Supreme Leader of All, Yes All, Robots? And because he's not terribly fond of . . . units . . . who look like . . . what you look like now? I'm not nervous."

Obi's robot face shifted into the equivalent of a smile as he shot out his paw, catching Beeps just as he was about to dent his third wall of the ride. "Definitely nervous."

"Zip it," Beeps barked.

With a sudden jerk, the elevator stopped and the door slid open—

*WHOOSSSSSSH.*

They were greeted with silence, except for the peaceful buzzing of the royal generators. The two robots moved through the elevator portal and into the hall, approaching the nearest guard.

Beeps rolled forward. "We're here to—"

*KWAKKKKRRRRRRGHHHHHHH!*

The rest of the sentence was obliterated by a strange

**27**

and horrible noise that echoed from down the hallway. Obi and Beeps looked at each other, confused.

The guard ignored the noise. "Follow me," the guard shouted, pivoting to lead them into the hall, where the noise only grew louder.

By the time they arrived at the Throne Room door, the obnoxious, distorted screeching was unbearable.

"Strange welcoming rituals you have here on Binar," Obi shouted, his voice barely audible over the dissonant, almost-violent sounds. "Is that music? Or some kind of torture?"

Beeps shot Obi a look—at first angry, then almost embarrassed. "It looks like . . . er, *sounds* like, the supreme leader has taken up electric guitar again." Beeps sighed. "The supreme leader is a fan of what the humans call rock and roll."

Obi stared. "I am very sorry to hear that. . . ."

Beeps nodded.

"Literally."

The door to the Throne Room slid open. Beeps winced. Obi took a step backward. "Definitely torture," he said to himself, as the sound grew louder still.

Inside, an elaborate elevated stage was surrounded by billowing fog in the center of the Throne Room. Dominating the stage was Robot AA-001, the one and only Supreme Leader of All, Yes All, Robots, SLAYAR himself. Color-changing spotlights lit SLAYAR from every direction, and his reflection was everywhere in the chrome-plated chamber—just as he liked it—like a real rock star.

*"DOMO ARIGATO, MR. ROBOTO, DOMO, DOMO!"*

He bellowed as he rotated through his favorite rock star poses and pointed to a nearby Royal Guard, who sang the chorus back to him, right on cue.

"DOMO!"

Then another.

"DOMO!"

And another.

"DOMOOOOO!"

But when the SLAYAR pointed again—this time to a guard standing directly in front of Beeps himself— Beeps responded by panicking and shoving Obi back out the door.

"Just w-wait here," Beeps said. "I'll h-handle it. You d-don't know what he can be like . . . when he's like . . . how he can b-be."

"Are you stuttering, Beeps?" Obi studied his captor-slash-host.

"N-no." Beeps banged his head with one grasper, then paused to adjust his audio sensitivity downward.

"I don't know why you let him behave like this," Obi

said. "For a society of AI-based units, it's not entirely logical."

"Can it, you," Beeps said. With that, he rolled bravely into the room to face the music, literally and figuratively.

Obi watched from the portal.

It was . . . a spectacle.

The smoke machines were going full blast, the rainbow spotlights, even the pyrotechnic displays. It seemed like some kind of grand finale, because now the high-platform stage was rising even higher and higher.

Obi saw Beeps pause before he rolled toward center stage.

SLAYAR's graspers ran up and down the neck of his electric guitar, and he frantically picked, plucked, and twanged the guitar's strings. Sparks flew in every direction.

On SLAYAR's main screen, where his face was usually displayed, Obi could only see a high-definition digital representation of hair—of long, flowing rock-and-roll locks—curls that swished and swayed as the supreme leader spun and maniacally bobbed his head up and down.

When SLAYAR noticed his number two in the room, the "music" came to a screeching halt.

Obi stepped back out of visual range, while he listened and waited.

He couldn't make out what the voices were saying specifically—but what seemed to start out as a quiet conversation quickly escalated into shouting, and then— CRASH!—Obi winced at what sounded like a shiny guitar smashing, followed by an awkward moment of regret and silent mourning of the smashed guitar.

"You!" A Royal Guard emerged from the door and barked at Obi. "This way."

The robo-cat followed the guard into the awkward silence.

Clink clink clink clink.

The foreign, tinny sound of his metal claws echoing off the chrome walls caught Obi off guard.

<< Nothing is as it was. This should not surprise me. >>

But the old cat-bot glimpsed his reflection in the polished-chrome walls as he headed into the room, and it did surprise him.

No matter.

Obi had something even bigger than getting used to his robotic body to worry about. Like, for example, offending the leader of a decidedly anti-cat nation, which could result in not having any sort of body at all.

*Clink clink clink clink. Clink.*

Obi slowly stepped through the dissipating fog, picking his way around the sparkly shattered bits of SLAYAR's shiny guitar.

Obi used every ounce of robotic willpower to avoid his cat urge to sniff each glittering piece, and then a few ounces more to keep from pouncing on the many tantalizing bouncing, bobbing guitar strings.

<< Some things never change. >>

SLAYAR was frantically searching for his favorite guitar pick in the wreckage, when he looked up and saw Obi walking through the portal door.

SLAYAR froze.

His digital mouth hung open at the sight of such a magnificent—if confusing—metal specimen.

"What. Is. That?" SLAYAR rolled toward the edge of the stage for a closer look. The Royal Guards stared from their posts. Even Beeps looked uncomfortable, swaying back and forth at the base of the stage.

"Come closer." The SLAYAR beckoned with a grasper.

*Clink clink clink clink.*

Obi kept walking as they all eyed him.

He wasn't sure what to make of it. The way their sensors never left him. The way they studied his motions, his mechanical articulations. He heard the words being whispered, here and there.

". . . mechanical masterwork . . ."

". . . a brilliant Maker . . ."

". . . clearly not Binar . . ."

". . . but robotic genius . . ."

". . . such expert design . . ."

". . . such craft . . ."

Obi watched them as intently as they were watching him. He knew the Binars were no fans of the Feline Empire, and he suspected he would have to rely on every available piece of information if he were to find a way off this planet.

<< Now I know the Wengrods made me well, even by Binar standards. That might help me get out of here in one piece, which is more than I can say for that SLAYAR fellow's poor electric guitar. . . . >>

As Obi approached, SLAYAR began babbling. He couldn't stop talking—and the rest of the room couldn't help listening.

"But . . . this is a wonder . . . the most graceful robot I've ever seen . . . stunning . . . And yet it is also somehow . . . revolting. I feel . . . an absolute revulsion . . . rising in my circuits. It is so . . . so . . . CAT-LIKE!"

Obi interrupted. "Yet I am a robot. A machine."

SLAYAR frowned. "But are you? Really?"

"He is," Beeps assured him.

"I am," Obi repeated, twisting his head all the way around on his neck roller.

"He is," the guards agreed, watching the head trick.

SLAYAR considered, tapping one metallic grasper against the other. "I'm torn . . . I admit it . . . I don't know whether to have this . . . *freak* . . . destroyed, or"—a smile emerged—"to invite him onstage to join my band. . . ."

"No, thank you," Obi said.

Beeps swallowed. "He means . . ."

"Silence!" SLAYAR said, not even looking at Beeps. "As much as I hate to admit it, this—what is the name of this model?"

"Obi," Beeps said.

SLAYAR nodded. "Obi is . . ."

The Royal Guards waited.

Beeps waited.

Even Obi wasn't sure where SLAYAR was going.

"Obi is . . . *FREAKING COOL!*"

The guards murmured and muttered in surprise.

Obi frowned.

Beeps looked around the room, speechless, as if it was all he could do not to ask, "*Is everyone else seeing this?*"

Only SLAYAR looked happy. He tried to hide it, but his smile grew wider, and it became clear to everyone in the room that SLAYAR had developed a ro-bro-crush on Obi . . .

. . . until SLAYAR noticed everyone staring at him and snapped right out of it.

"Er, I mean, freaking cool . . . for a . . . *FREAKY CAT THING!*" SLAYAR kept his eyes glued on Obi. "Beeps, you say the Singularity Chip we were looking for is inside . . . this *FREAKY CAT-THING . . . ABOMINATION?*"

"Guilty as charged," Obi answered calmly.

Beeps rolled nervously into a chunk of guitar.

"The Singularity Chip is indeed implanted and fused into my systems." Obi leaped effortlessly onto the stage, to give everyone a better look.

"I should also note that my consciousness, my memories, all the experiences of my nine lives, have been similarly implanted and permanently fused into the Singularity Chip."

Obi turned to reveal the small glowing cube inside him.

Excitement rippled through the room.

The robo-cat continued. "You might say we are an inseparable pair. It's a bit complex, and rather cutting-edge. I'm afraid there's no other creature, technology, or being anywhere in the galaxy quite like me. *Singular,* you see?"

<< A calculated strategy. CAT-SPLAINING and ROBO-SPLAINING to SLAYAR. The biggest of no-no's. Hopefully. >>

Obi was banking on the possibility—or rather, the high probability—that anyone with a rock-star-sized ego might have an issue with not being the *singular* main attraction, or not even knowing how that singular main attraction worked.

<< Irritate an inflated ego and hope he wants to send me away, or even back. >>

"WHATEVER!"

SLAYAR slammed his graspers into the stage, startling Obi. The mechanical cat leaped gracefully back down to land at Beeps's side, below the stage.

"You"—SLAYAR pointed at Obi—"don't talk in riddles and don't treat the SUPREME LEADER like an eight-bit moron!"

<< Here we go. A dangerous game, for a fellow on his tenth life. If that's even how I can count this one? >>

"I'm so sor . . ." Obi began.

"Zip it!" Beeps hissed, cutting him off.

SLAYAR glared at both robots.

"I've had enough of this. Just give me the chip. NOW."

"Unfortunately, Your Shininess, what the—the Obi said is true." Beeps hesitated. "The chip has been, er, permanently merged into his . . . the FREAKING CAT ABOMINATION THING's . . . body."

Obi smiled.

It felt good to smile, even a mechanical one.

"Impossible?" SLAYAR growled. "Oh, I believe anything's possible . . . with the right motivation. Don't you agree, Beeps?"

He gestured with one grasper, and the lights dimmed.

In the center of the chamber, a holographic image appeared. A desolate black mountain bellowing red-tinged smoke.

The Royal Guards reacted with shock.

The holograph changed, the view zooming inward and upward, until Obi could see a gaping crater full of bubbling lava, giant rising geysers of magma, spilling and oozing down the sides of the mountain.

SLAYAR's voice called out from the stage. "Recognize this, Beeps?"

Beeps couldn't believe his eye. "You can't be serious, sir."

"What is it?" Obi whispered.

Beeps was panicking. "I knew SLAYAR was angry, but I didn't expect him to threaten Slag Mountain."

"Slag Mountain?" Obi knew it didn't sound good.

Beeps couldn't seem to move his eyes from the terrible glow of the holograph. "Slag Mountain. The Great

Recycler. The heat so great that no known metal had ever survived it. No punishment is more feared on Binar than being Slagged. . . ."

"Oh, Beeps." Obi was really starting to feel for the strange rolly fellow.

"Well, Beeps?" SLAYAR interrupted again. "You have one week to get that chip out of the CAT THING— or, I guess, the CAT THING out of the chip—or whatever, you know what I mean!"

"I really don't," Beeps said.

"Well, I do," SLAYAR snapped. He was clearly flustered. "Fail me, and *both* of you get a ONE-WAY TICKET TO SLAG CITY!"

Even the guards twitched with fear at the threat. "Slag City?!"

Beeps looked like he was going to fall over.

Obi surreptitiously extended one metallic paw, righting him more solidly on his wheel. Just in case. They'd had enough dings and dents for one day, the two of them.

He shook his head, or rather pivoted it a bit.

This SLAYAR had demanded the impossible of both himself and his captor, and something equally impossible had happened: their survival, or their doom, had become permanently linked.

Obi and Beeps.

Robot and Robo-Cat alike.

SLAYAR brought the lights back up and stared at both of them—wild-eyed, full of rage. Beeps took one look and began to roll toward the Throne Room exit portal as quickly as he could, dragging Obi along after him.

The two robots didn't speak until they were safely inside the elevator again.

"We need to figure something out," Beeps finally said.

*Kkrinkkk-krinkkk.*

Obi's tail twitched, clink-scraping against the chrome floor. The sound was unnerving, which was how he felt.

"We need something, indeed."

What did they need?

What did one do, on the verge of a great Slagging?

Obi felt a surge in his circuits as he thought again of his faraway Furless planet home. He wondered if Max would know what to do. Max, or Min.

If they would be worried. If they were, now.

He thought of the ever-irritating kittens . . . the kindly faced Javi . . . even the metal-head Protos prompted a strange sensation of longing . . .

. . . *of family.*

That was what they had been to him. That was what they had taught him. Obi could do anything, but he could not do it alone.

<< That's it, then. I need to speak with Pounce.

He'll know what to do. >>

Obi lifted a rubber-capped paw and touched the medallion still around his neck. He could use it, but only at great risk; the Binars knew his medallion functioned as a translator, but what they didn't yet realize was that it was also a transmitter capable of communicating at great distances . . .

. . . even as great as the distance between Binar and the planet Felinus, seat of the Great Feline Empire . . . and home of his old friend Pounce.

Obi would need to find an excuse for some kind of privacy if he wanted to use his medallion to secretly call for help. . . .

Because he did want help. For himself, and for his odd and anxious newfound companion. Because they shared one thing, at least, in common . . .

They very much did not wish to be Slagged.

Obi sighed.

<< Pounce, old friend, I do hope you can figure out how to get me out of here. >>

# 4

## Woe Is Meow

**A**cross the galaxy, on the planet Felinus, a rather bulky Chairman Meow fidgeted atop his sprawling throne. The grand structure dominated the Throne Room and looked like the most elaborate, spectacular cat tower imaginable.

Meow twitched and scratched.

With great effort, the prime leader of the Great Feline Empire rolled his enormous orange body this way and that, unable to get comfortable. The chairman wanted to nap, but today, like most days of late, he was consumed with thoughts of life and death.

Meow, a ruddy Abyssinian shorthair, was well into his ninth life, and as each day passed, he worried that it might be his last. His concern grew with every newly shed, snow-colored hair that floated down from his throne.

Giving up on rest, Meow growled as he twisted onto his belly and set his head down on his two front paws, looking down from his perch on the eleventh level of his beloved throne. He quickly spotted his familiar nemesis— a mysterious glint of light that bounced and jumped around on the floor far below.

During his early lives, Meow was known to hunt the light relentlessly, sometimes spending entire *minutes* bounding around the Throne Room.

The light always returned, much to Meow's annoyance.

"I will catch you," Meow said quietly . . . but inside he wondered if he had enough time left, even to hunt the light.

He sighed.

Meow's ear twitched as a faint but familiar tapping sound interrupted his dejected thoughts. As it grew louder, he recognized the off-beat tapping as the footsteps of his second-in-command, Pounce de Leon.

Pounce's right forepaw had one stubborn claw that would never fully retract and poked slightly through his paw. For his entire lives (eight, so far), the claw tapped against the floor as he walked—an irregularity that made it impossible for him to sneak properly and, unfortunately, had thus invited a fair amount of bullying as a kitten.

"Finally," Meow said, heaving himself up just as Pounce entered the room; the dignified-looking tuxedo cat seemed a bit tired and more tentative than usual, which was not a good sign.

Pounce was also alone, which was an even worse sign.

As it registered that Pounce had arrived empty-pawed, Meow's heart sunk.

Pounce had been sent on a critical mission to Earth to recover a rare invention that, Meow had hoped, would solve his pesky problem with mortality.

Dispirited, Meow dispensed with formalities and asked the obvious question.

"Where is my, um, you know, that thing that I sent you to get—what was it called?" Meow's grasp of the finer details was steadily fading with the years.

"Singularity Chip, Your Furness," Pounce said wearily. "Did you not get my messages? I sent multiple detailed after-action reports describing the encounter on Earth."

"Not one."

Pounce paused and nervously licked a spot that was already quite clean. *"At least I think I did,"* he said to himself quietly. As one of the few truly organized cats in the empire, he was well versed in pretending to blame himself for the poor executive skills of others.

Meow gave an indignant hiss. "I never read those things, you know that!"

Pounce leaped up onto the lowest level of the throne, hoping to get a better view of his leader as he broke the news. "Well, to be brief, Chairman—I'm sorry to say that the mission was a failure. Mostly."

"Mostly?" Meow moaned.

*RAWRRRR.*

"How can you mostly fail?"

Pounce tried to put a bold face on. "Well, the good news is I saw the Singularity Chip successfully used to extend a brave GFE soldier's existence beyond his ninth life. You remember Obi? Our agent on Earth. . . ."

Meow's ears perked up at the news, a faint spark of hope in his increasingly clouded eyes. "Wonderful! And of course I remember," Meow said, of course not remembering. "Brave soul, that Obi. So happy to hear he's well."

"Quite well, sir. Although"—Pounce hesitated—"he was required to take on . . . a particularly *robot-like* form. . . ." There was no easy way to say it. "But by all

**44**

accounts he is, or I should say was, very much alive and well."

"Robot-like?" Meow howled, hopes dashed again. *"Was?"*

He rolled onto his back exasperated, legs flopping and limp. His old heart couldn't take much more of this emotional roller coaster. (Either that, or the seventy-four anchovies he'd eaten at breakfast were not sitting well with him.)

Pounce paced in circles, trying to spit out the bad news. "Obi's original body had been worn down, quite unsustainable. And the invention, the chip, does require the subject to . . . *migrate* . . . to a new robotic form."

"Ew! Disgusting!" Meow exclaimed to the ceiling, then paused to consider. "How did it look?"

"Quite impressive, actually. Highly mobile, strong, capable. Cat-like—in almost every way." Pounce smiled. "I could use a bit of robot myself, particularly in the left hip, at least on rainy days . . ."

"Maybe a robot body wouldn't be so bad," Meow mused.

"Before you go further with that thought," Pounce interrupted, "the chip is permanently attached to Obi's body. It is Obi, in a way, and can't be used again."

The chairman hissed with annoyance. "Seriously? Such a rare opportunity and they WASTED it on what's-his-name? At least bring him in so I can take a look," Meow said.

"I'm afraid that's not possible." Pounce winced and braced himself as he revealed the final bit of news, the piece that had been troubling him most of all. "I'm sorry to say that Obi was taken by the Binars. Back to their home planet."

"Whatever for?"

"At best, to be examined. Thoroughly. At worst? Quite possibly taken apart . . . permanently."

Pounce could hardly stand to think about it. He found himself staring at his collar communicator at all hours of the day and night, pacing the length of the palace, wondering what to do. If he reached out at the wrong time, he knew he could get Obi into even more trouble. But if he didn't reach out *in time,* well, it could be too late to help his friend at all.

"On my ninth and final life," Meow gasped, and nearly rolled off his platform in despair, "they're going to destroy *the chip?*"

"*And* Obi," Pounce said diplomatically. "Most likely, yes." He arched his back and scratched at the throne, because sometimes that's all a cat can do.

After an awkward moment of silence, the massive orange lump on the throne stirred. "Pounce de Leon," Meow said as he heaved himself upright, as dignified as possible. "You have served me loyally for many lives, but this failure is unacceptable."

"Yes, Your Meowjesty," Pounce said, head low.

"I need the chip. And, yes, if it must be, a robot body. I don't have much time, which means you have even less. I am giving you one week to correct this." He looked down at Pounce, angry and desperate. "Fail me, and I will have no choice but to make an example of you . . . and *banish you* from the Great Feline Empire."

Pounce froze, ears twitching.

Banishment would be a death sentence for a cat like Pounce, who was a decidedly indoors, in-Empire type of cat. He paced in a tight circle, panic building. "What would you have me do, Chairman?"

"How should I know?" the old cat wheezed. "Make a new one. Create a time machine and go back and fix this mess. Whatever it takes," he gasped dramatically, struggling as he coughed up an ancient hairball. . . .

"Just GO!"

\* 🙰 \*

*I've never seen the chairman so furr-ious!*

The sight of Meow in such a state startled Pounce. As he trotted—and tapped—away from the Throne

Room, he tried to compose himself, but inside he was full of furry worry.

It was time to risk making the call.

He needed to talk to Obi.

He pawed at his medallion collar to activate it—and was still preparing to send a waiting signal—when a familiar voice sounded on the other end of the collar communicator. "Pounce, is that you?"

*Obi.*

The tuxedo cat looked startled, then relieved. "Obi, thank goodness, are you safe?"

"For now—but not for long. I've managed to give Beeps the slip, but we don't have much time to talk." Obi's voice was low. "Things are bad, old friend."

Pounce sighed. "We've got trouble here as well, Obi. I'm afraid Chairman Meow will stop at nothing to get you and the chip."

Obi's reply crackled through the medallion: "You haven't seen insanity until you've seen SLAYAR angry. I tried to get him to send me back . . . but instead he's threatened to throw Beeps and me into some horrible lava-filled mountain of doom if we don't give him the chip."

"We can't give them what they want," Pounce said, reality sinking in. "Either one of them. We're both doomed."

"It appears that way," Obi agreed. "It also seems likely that they won't stop at punishing us, or the Empire. All of this may just be the beginning of something even worse."

"True," Pounce said. "Meow will almost certainly order an attack on Binar to get the chip."

"SLAYAR will attack Earth to get a new one," Obi continued.

Pounce was grim. "They could end up destroying each other, and everything we hold dear. Even the Furless planet."

"Earth," Obi said, sounding sad. "My Furless friends. My found family. They're what I hold most dear now. I find my mind going back there, when I least expect it."

"Ah, yes. I remember. Your Max . . . The Boy."

"His sister too," Obi admitted. "I'm afraid they grow on you, like that. The Furless. You don't see it coming, of course. Don't know how much you're going to care . . ."

"I suppose not."

"But then, in a blink, it's just gone. And you find . . . to your great surprise . . . oh, you cared, Pounce. You cared quite a bit indeed." Obi's voice, if a bit tinny in tone, was thick with emotion.

"I did? Or you did?" Pounce echoed, a bit confused.

"It doesn't matter. That's the whole point. Everyone does."

"Ah." Pounce finally understood. "You've gone soft, old man."

"Perhaps." Obi sighed. "You know, in your ninth go, things begin to get . . . sentimental. You realize you've gotten used to it, to the spin and the size of it, the routine and the weather of it, really."

"The weather of what?"

"Of your life. Of the buzz of it, of the living things in it. You start to crave that kind of warm, messy, laundry-day noise. Nothing important. Nothing new. Just the . . . well, the *purr* of it all, I suppose. The purr and the pulse. Take it from a creature who no longer has either."

"I don't believe—"

"You will remember it all, Pounce. And you will miss it. You will miss them. Even when they're as irritating as two Dumpster kittens who get under your paws—and a flying thingamajig that buzzes in your face with her broken propeller."

"Please. Joan Drone has impeccable judgment."

"I suppose it's a bit like a tail you can never catch, or a great ball of yarn that never quite unravels all the way, no matter how hard you chase it. You can't win, and the further along you get, the less you want to—because that would mean it's over. And the game was—well, it was everything, Pounce. You'll see."

*Will I?*

Pounce shivered. He knew the old cat's perspective was every bit as singular as the chip that had brought him back to life.

Obi's was a voice from beyond the ninth. He was a singular tenth. Transformed.

And this Obi *One-Two* Catnobi had seen more than any other cat in the history of the Great Feline Empire.

*Will I be so dignified, when my game ends?*

Unable to resolve the nature of existence, Obi returned to the pressing matters of the moment. "We need to contact the Furless inventors, the Wengrods. They understand how the Singularity Chip works, as they invented it. Perhaps they can help."

"I agree," Pounce said. "I'll take care of it. You do what you must to stay safe, old friend."

"Easier said than done, in this strange place," Obi answered. "But I promise to try. We cannot let things fall apart without trying. That is all any of us can do."

Pounce nodded. "You always were a strange creature, and I'm afraid you've only gotten stranger, but I believe I quite like it, the Tenth Obi." By the time he finished the sentence, the Cat of Ten Lives was gone.

Pounce stress-yawned—as any cat would, when all appeared to be very nearly lost—and curled up to take a restorative nap.

He found he was exhausted, every bit of him. Mind

and heart and soul. Talking to Obi had made Pounce . . .
aware. That was the only way he could describe it, the
whole of it.

*The purr of it,* he thought. *Maybe the old Tenth was
right.*

As Pounce started to doze, problems circled around
his thoughts like butterflies.

*The humans started this conflict and brought us all
into it.*

*Now they need to fix it.*

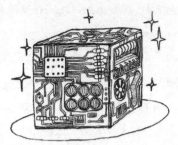

# 5

## A New Hope?

**"T**here's only one hundred and four days of summer vacation," Max said. "It's going so quickly. How is it we still haven't heard from Pounce?"

It was the end of another long summer day, which meant the twins had crashed noisily inside, following their ritual of snacking, flopping, and moaning about wasting precious summertime. As usual, Javi had taken a break from preparing their big case to join Max and Min for their customary pickle chips and juice packs.

"We still haven't figured out how we can help Obi,"

Min said. Unsolved problems frustrated her, whether or not they were her own.

"At least your folks are home today," Javi said encouragingly. "Maybe you can all hang out."

"They're probably too busy," Max said glumly. "As usual."

The twins had hardly seen their parents all summer, since the two Drs. Wengrod had either been sequestered in their own lab, or away touring labs, as they worked around the clock to undo everything the renegade House had done to compromise their many classified works in progress.

Max knew he couldn't really complain. If anybody knew how important their parents' work was, it was Max and Min. After all, without the Wengrods' work, there wouldn't be a Singularity Chip at all, and Obi would have . . . Max didn't even want to think about it.

But even so, parents who were busy doing important *work* things sometimes didn't have time to do important *parent* things. This summer, Max and Min had been left to process everything that had happened, for the most part, on their own.

Lately, that had felt sort of unfair—even if letting himself feel the *unfair* feeling had also made Max feel the *guilty* feeling that came right after it.

He sighed. "I think I need a Capri Sun."

＊ 🞶 ＊

As Max and Min spoke, Joan Drone darted back and forth between the family and the kitchen, dropping snacks and juice packs like guided missiles.

Capri Suns. *Check.*

Fruit snacks. *Check.*

Pickle chips. *Check.*

Once the supplies had been satisfactorily delivered, she buzzed around the room one last time to make certain everything was in order.

"Mess duties completed. Commence perimeter security check!" Joan barked into her comms. "North side?"

"North side clear!" Drags shouted as he peered through the screen door. "Like always."

Joan chided him. "Negative, Drags. Not like always. If we had executed regular security checks, we might have caught a major security breach in our own headquarters as it was happening."

She had taken the House betrayal more personally than any of the others, and had sworn to never let something like that happen again.

Not on her watch.

"East side?"

Cy looked out the window to the low stone wall at the edge of the Wengrods' driveway, where Obi had sat for so many years in his furry form. "East side c-c-clear!"

"South side?" Joan waited.

Nothing.

She tried again. "Tipsy, do you have eyes on the south side perimeter?"

Static.

Now Joan was frustrated—and, however irrationally, worried. "Are you there, Tipsy? The back lawn? Is everything okay back there?"

"I'll go check," Drags said.

"I can," Cy said.

But another burst of static came, and with it an enormous delighted laugh.

"Birdies!" Tipsy shouted gleefully. "Birdies back there!"

Joan nodded a propeller with relief. Of course. There was nothing Tipsy liked so much as watching the red hummingbird feeder that hung from the avocado tree in the Wengrods' overgrown backyard.

She switched back on her comms. "Thank you, Tipsy. Perimeter check complete. Let's rendezvous in the lab and power down for a power nap."

As Joan Drone flew past the family room bookshelves, she noticed a small speck on the kittens' pet cam. When she swept back around for another look, the speck had disappeared.

*Hmmm*, she thought as she returned to the lab. She set a second—then a third—evening reminder to do a more thorough check of their interior headquarters later.

*A Proto couldn't be too careful.*

Not since they'd discovered the AI traitor in their own *House*.

It had been a real eye-opener.

Even if you didn't happen to have eyes of your own.

The door to the family robotics lab swung open. The twins' parents, Dr. and Dr. Wengrod—or, Mom and Dad—emerged into the kitchen, smiling.

"Where are my hugs?" Mom said cheerfully. Max and Min responded with a chorus of tired grunts in return.

Javi waved.

Dad sat down next to Min, sneakily snatching one of her chips. "Rough day at the internship office, huh?"

"My brain is so tired I feel like I've run a marathon and all I did was sit in a chair all day staring at a screen," Min said, crumpling up her empty chip bag. Scout leaped up onto the table and stuck her head inside the bag. Investigating.

"At least you got something done. The only thing I've learned about building video games this summer is that they're basically always broken, like, at least ninety percent of the time," Max said, scratching Stu's ears.

Stu flickered open one eye, following his sister as she crawled halfway inside the pickle chip bag. He closed it.

Mom sat down between Max and Stu and gave both boys—furred and furless—a good head scratch.

Stu purred. Max grinned. "That tickles . . . Don't stop."

Mom smiled. "One more scratch, and then we should have a team meeting, don't you think? We need to talk about Obi."

Max, Min, and Javi looked at the Drs. Wengrod.

"Finally," Max said.

"We've been going crazy not doing anything," Min said.

"How can we help?" Javi asked.

Dad looked serious. "I don't know, but it's time we brainstormed something. Our lab server just picked up some kind of involuntary ping from the Singularity Chip. Obi seems to be sending a distress signal."

"Distress signal?" Max yelped.

"We don't know it's for us. Just that he's . . . in distress," Mom said.

"Hold up." Javi motioned to Max, whispering, "Is it

even safe to talk . . . about that . . . here? What about House . . . and all that snooping spyware?"

Max looked around the kitchen suspiciously.

"Mom and Dad got rid of all that," Min said. Then she looked at her parents. "Didn't you?"

* 🔯 *

Over the bookshelf, the Roachbot was creeping back into position on the pet cam but immediately froze when it heard the words *House* and *spyware*.

Its tiny sensors lit up red.

<<HOUSE: TRIGGER PROTOCOL>>

<<SPYWARE: TRIGGER PROTOCOL>>

<<ASSESSING: MISSION VIABILITY>>

<<MAINTAIN>>

The Roachbot scanned the room.

No further threats emerged.

Its sensors faded back to white again.

<<REVISED PROTOCOL: NORMAL>>

And with that, the Roachbot zipped back on top of the pet cam and started broadcasting again.

Which was when Joan Drone flew slowly into the room . . .

* 🔯 *

"I'm still freaked out even thinking about creepy old House bossing us around, listening to everything we say." Min ripped open her second bag of pickle chips.

Max lay on the floor, his face buried in Stu's chubby kitten belly.

Scout sat nearby, ignoring them. She was too busy investigating—eyeing Joan Drone as she hovered in front of the bookshelves.

"I know, I know, that was our fault," Dad admitted, stealing some of Min's chips. "We thought House would be helpful when we went to China, but we've learned our lesson."

"That's right," Mom said. "It's taken a monthlong search-and-destroy mission to remove every trace of the House code from our home, but we now have a *House-free* house!"

"So if we aren't being spied on," Min said, "why are you both always down in the lab?"

Min had been her father's right hand for a long time. She knew her father well enough to know when something was going on.

Like now.

And Min's father knew her well enough to know how hurt she was when he didn't let her in on his tech experiments.

Also like now.

"The Singularity Chip integrated more successfully with Obi's neural network and the robotic prosthesis than we ever could have hoped. Because of that, when Beeps ran off with Obi and our chip, we decided not to retrace our steps, but to build something even bigger and better," Dad said.

"You mean, you've been in the lab working on Singularity Chip two point oh?" Min asked. "I knew it!"

"That's cool," Max said.

"Seriously," Javi agreed.

"Well, we had a little help from an old friend," Mom said mysteriously.

"Who?" Min said, sounding a little jealous.

"We call it the Infinity Engine. And believe me," Dad said, "this thing makes the Singularity Chip seem like . . . a potato chip."

"Infinity Engine?" Min liked the sound of that.

"Potato chips?" Max realized he hadn't had lunch.

"Wow," Javi said. "That sounds . . . powerful."

"It is!" Mom nodded, excited. "We improved the design of the quantum energy source, and the power it can generate is unbelievable."

Max stared at the ceiling, getting bored. "Got it. It's like the chip but way better."

"Way better?" Mom raised an eyebrow at Max. "Sure, if by *way better* you mean *expanded processing capabilities so advanced they might exceed the capacity of the human brain."*

"Uh, yeah, that's what I meant." Max grinned, sheepish.

＊ ⋈ ＊

Scout stared up at the bookshelves. Something was going on up there. She was sure of it.

"Would you just relax already?" Stu was rolling on the floor next to Max.

"No, I won't relax." Scout sniffed. "Relaxing is how that evil House almost destroyed this entire family, or have you forgotten already?"

"I'm just saying. The Furless seem to have it under control."

"Stu, Obi almost died, now he's gone, and there's a war between our own people and machines. Nobody has anything under control." Scout began to do what she always did when she was super stressed out, which was briskly scratch her right ear with her bottom left foot.

"Fine. You do you." Stu tucked all four paws beneath him, morphing into his favorite cat loaf position. He buried his face in his chest until he looked like a bit like a stuffed, furry brick.

"I will," Scout said, prowling around the lower

bookshelves. "I just wish I could see . . . a little . . . higher . . . up there."

"Do not do the shelf thing," Stu warned, his voice muffled by fur and whiskers.

"I don't have a *shelf thing*," Scout hissed back at him.

"Scout. You totally have a shelf thing." More fur and whiskers.

Scout snorted, still eyeing the shelves. "I mean, *maybe* there was that one time in Min's room, but that was as much *your* shelf thing as it was *my* shelf thing, Stuart."

"Don't say I didn't warn you."

"Don't you have to get back to your *nap thing?*"

Scout moved away, prowling around the lower bookshelves. She couldn't see the higher shelves, but couldn't not keep trying to. . . .

Before she knew it, she was wiggling her butt, trying to gauge the jump up, getting ready to throw herself into it—even if it seemed too far.

Scout sat back on her haunches, considering her options as kitten math kicked in: *Ottoman to chair to shelf. Stereo speaker to coffee table to plant to shelf. Wooden armchair to middle shelf . . .*

Ding ding ding! That one. Wooden armchair.

And so she began to scramble up onto the armchair with all the confidence of a kitten with a *shelf thing*.

Max watched Scout climb onto the chair, but he didn't stop her. The family meeting had grown too serious to be interrupted.

"We can't scan a human brain yet," Dad continued, "but there are a lot of complex things the brain does that we already know how to code up but are too complex for any mobile robot to perform."

"Like what?" Max asked.

"If you think about it," Dad said, "a lot of what a brain does is predictable, almost mechanical, like moving your body."

"You mean motor skills?" Min said.

"Exactly." Mom smiled. "Walking, running, balancing, controlling your arms and hands, those are things programmers have solved, but take too much processing to calculate quickly enough."

"Like Elmer's walking algorithm!" Min said, excited.

"Exactly. Elmer's programming works, but it's slow and still has problems. With the Infinity Engine, we can finally make a robot that could process everything quickly enough to handle movement as well as a human, maybe better."

Javi listened intently. "I can imagine a lot of ways to

use something like this. It could help a lot of people."

Dad looked excited too. "Even just as a power source, if we can figure out how to mass-produce it, we could help people power their homes or cars without polluting. Clean, cheap, and portable energy."

"It could power and guide an exoskeleton so people with disabilities could take care of themselves, walk, move, drive, almost anything." Min's mind was racing.

"We're talking the future of robotic movement— light-years beyond anything anyone has seen or even imagined," Mom said.

Max stared across the room, watching Scout sit at attention in a wooden armchair, balancing herself with great care, to stare at something only she could see.

"It's hard to imagine things before you can see them," Max said.

✳ ◁◯▷ ✳

Scout balanced herself carefully along the wooden arm of the chair. She stretched and craned her furry neck, desperately scanning the shelf.

She didn't know why she was driven to investigate one particular shelf and not another. There was always a reason. Some tiny motion that shouldn't be there. A shape that didn't belong. A sound that hadn't been there in the past.

Something wrong, in the wrong place, at the wrong time, making the wrong sound or the wrong smell. Any one of a number of tiny *details of wrongness* that seemed so unimportant to anyone else, and yet so critically . . . *investigation-worthy* . . . to a kitten.

*THERE!*

She froze in place, ears twitching.

On the little white box—their tiny white box, the one Max sometimes would use to, she didn't know, hide inside and talk to them—she saw a tiny creature.

A oval-shaped black spot thing, with lots of legs.

A BUG.

That was what Max had called it.

But a particular kind of bug—not the flying and buzzing kind—rather the scuttling and crawling kind.

The kind she usually only saw downstairs in the basement, when all the lights were off.

But this wasn't the basement.

And these lights were definitely not off.

And yet there it was, sitting there, right out in the open.

So this wasn't just a BUG.

It was the WRONG BUG.

And that meant one thing: KITTEN GO TIME!

Scout carefully turned to face the shelf.

*Can I make that jump?*

She took a deep breath.

*Do I have a choice?*

✳ 🐱 ✳

Max turned back from Scout to listen to his mom talking.

"The engine could enable intelligent and reliable robotic space exploration, long journeys into deep space, or dangerous ones, where humans wouldn't survive," Mom said. "We could also design AI or remote-controlled robots for search and rescue operations."

"Yeah, the engine generates enough power to do superhero kinds of things, like lifting heavy rocks or concrete," Dad said.

"Flying?" Min asked.

Mom shrugged. "If we designed the right thrusters, sure."

"Lifting cars, punching through walls?" Max chimed in.

"With the right mechanical design, no problem," Dad said. "All the Iron Man stuff."

"What about shooting lasers?" Max wondered.

Min scoffed, but looked like even she still wanted to know the answer.

"Maybe," Mom said, "but we don't want the engine to be used as a weapon to hurt peop—"

*RAWRRRRR!*

"What the—" Max turned just in time to catch a glimpse of Scout launching off the back of the chair toward the bookshelf.

Stu sat up as the chair tipped toward him—

Scout went flying into the shelf—

*CRASSSSHHHHHHH!*

*YOWWWWWLLLL!*

The chair went tumbling—

Stu shot out of the room.

\* ⋈ \*

In all the ruckus, nobody noticed as a small black mechanical insect detached from the pet cam and slipped away into the shadows behind it.

Had anyone been watching, they would have noticed a tiny green sensor lighting up next to the single word: "AUDIO."

\* ⋈ \*

"Scout, what are you doing?" Javi jumped over to pick the trembling kitten up from the bookshelf. "Have you gone loco? Shelves are for books, not kittens."

Max held out his hands for Scout, but she clawed at him when he tried to take her. "Just let her go. She's probably just freaked herself out.

Javi set Scout down.

She streaked away, fleeing the scene of the crime for the immediate hallway.

*That's weird,* thought Max. *She usually disappears after a big shelf-wreck. It's almost like she's actually worried about something.*

But then he stopped thinking about it, because his pocket was buzzing.

*BZZZZZZZZ.*

*BZZZZZZZZ.*

He pulled out his phone, but the buzzing continued.

"Oh!" Max jumped up. "Everybody, look!"

He fished in his pocket until he pulled out Pounce's medallion, placing it on the table. Min leaned over the communicator next to him. Javi and Mom and Dad gathered around to see the medallion glowing, pulsing, coming alive.

The faint buzzing grew louder—and the medallion grew brighter—then grew still.

Suddenly, there was a crackle of static, then a distant voice projecting from the medallion:

"GREETINGS FROM FELINUS!"

*Crackle.*

"POUNCE HERE!"

*Crackle.*

"SAY, CAN ANYONE HEAR ME?"

# 6

## Plotting with Pounce

"**W**e hear you! We hear you, Pounce! Can you hear us?" Max shouted into the medallion. His sister and family were gathered around, and now even Stu and Scout were climbing up onto the table to see what all the fuss was about.

Min plugged her ears and glared. "Max, you don't have to shout!"

"But it's long distance!" Max said, still shouting.

"Min is correct, I can hear you quite well without raising your voice." Pounce's voice grew clearer as he spoke. "If you don't mind."

Max rolled his eyes, but he cut right to the chase. He wanted to know the answer to the one question that mattered most of all:

"What about Obi? Is he okay? Have you heard from Obi?!"

Min's eyes met his as they waited for an answer.

Pounce began to speak—but static erupted over the words—which then faded out. It seemed for a moment like they'd lost the connection entirely.

Now it was Min who was shouting. "Pounce?! Pounce can you hear us?! What about Obi?"

But a moment later, Pounce's voice cut right through the static.

"Obi's fine—yes, yes—terrible connection—but fine, at least for now."

Everyone let out a sigh of relief as Pounce continued.

"But I'm afraid both of us are in trouble. Meow is furious that the Binars have taken Obi. SLAYAR is furious that Obi has permanently fused with the chip. Neither has gotten what they wanted—and it looks like Obi and I are likely to end up paying the price."

The words were ominous and hung over the Wengrods' kitchen table. Stu flattened his ears. Scout glared at the glowing medallion with suspicion.

"I don't like the sound of that," Dad said, speaking toward the medallion.

"In a way, we are the victims of your success with the chip," Pounce said. "SLAYAR wants his source of eternal power, and Meow, who has reached the end of his ninth life, hopes it can save him from oblivion, just as it saved Obi."

Javi nodded, frowning. "Not to mention that they're probably also worried the other side will get it first and use it to their advantage."

"Correct. Both leaders are competitive, stubborn, and won't accept that the chip in Obi is useless to them." Pounce sounded defeated. "I have nothing to offer Meow, and SLAYAR may not stop until he's taken Obi apart entirely. We just can't give them what they want. I'm afraid we're both quite done for, it seems."

"What if we made new chips for them?" Min asked hopefully.

Dad scratched Stu behind the ears as he thought. "We lost a lot of data when House corrupted our network, and had to wipe the network clean. I don't think we could make more anytime soon."

"But," Mom said, "maybe we can offer them something better?"

Max and Min looked at her. Pounce remained silent.

"The Infinity Engine?" Dad raised an eyebrow.

"The what?" Pounce said.

"It's a long story," Min said, leaning in to the medallion,

"but it's something my mom and dad are building that's way more powerful than the Singularity Chip."

"It's not quite finished, but it would be faster than making new chips," Dad said. "I don't know how we would get it to them, though."

"I think it's worth a shot," Mom said. "I can't think of a better idea."

"Whatever this engine is," Pounce said, an edge of worry in his voice, "it's better than what we have now, which is nothing."

An awkward silence fell back upon the room.

Max slumped in a kitchen chair, disappointed. "This is bad. What's going to happen to Obi? We don't even know how to get him back from Binar."

"We will do everything we can from here to keep Obi safe from the lava. And me, from exile," Pounce said, sounding dismal. "Considering the impatience of SLAYAR and Meow, that's all we can do. But we don't have much time."

Max put his head in his hands. "What if it's not enough?"

"I will tell Obi about the engine. Maybe it can help. Good luck to us all. Pounce out." Then, hesitating: "One more thing, Furless family. Your Obi cares about you a great deal. I can't say it the way he did, but he . . . misses you. I believe his exact words were that . . . you

**74**

were . . . everything. If we don't . . . if he doesn't . . . well, I thought you should know, is all."

A whole galaxy away, an aging cat found himself clearing his throat, as though it was suddenly thick with a fur ball that wasn't made of fur at all . . .

"Pounce out."

The medallion's glow dimmed as the speaker went silent.

The room was silent as well.

Max wiped his eyes, which were starting to burn with affection and emotion and any other word he could think of except for what it really was, which were tears.

Min put her head down on the kitchen table, openly weeping.

Mom and Dad looked at each other.

It was Javi who finally spoke, breaking the tension. "Well, no use moping about what we can't change—let's break this problem down and see what we can fix."

"That's what Obi would say." Max smiled, wiping his wet nose with the back of his hand. Min sat up, rubbing her face with her sweatshirt sleeve.

"That's right," Dad said. "So where do we begin?"

Javi jumped up. "I know how to get this party started." They loved a brainstorm session, and they *especially* loved one that involved solving complex international—or even better, intergalactic—problems.

Javi also knew how to keep the twins interested, and before anyone could complain about being tired, they rolled a massive whiteboard out from the lab.

"Yes!" Max loved whiteboards.

He immediately gathered all the colored dry-erase markers he could find and claimed an open space in the corner.

Before the brainstorming could even begin, he had already started doodling what looked like an insect army at war.

Nobody stopped him. The Wengrods all knew that it was how Max could think best, with a marker in his hand.

The rest of the whiteboard was full of lists and notes. Min came closer and looked at Javi, eyebrow raised. "How come you *already* have a plan, Javi?"

"I've done some work on this in my spare time," Javi said sheepishly, snatching back a black marker from Max.

"Just trying to get a handle on things. Sometimes when you have a problem that seems impossible," Javi said, "it helps to break that problem into smaller pieces that are easier to figure out." Javi, enjoying this "teaching moment," turned the board so everyone could read it.

## JAVI'S BIG BREAKDOWN OF BIG PROBLEMS
**Problem 1:** Rescue Obi from Binar—in one piece!
**Solution:** Go to Binar?

**Obstacles:** Where the heck is Binar? How do we get to Binar?

**Problem 2:** Keep Cats & Robots from fighting.
**Solution A:** Diplomacy? Plead with leaders?
**Obstacles:** Can we even talk to their leaders? Will they listen?
**Solution B:** Bargaining? Give them . . . Infinity Engine?
**Obstacles:** Can we finish it in time? How do we get it to them?

**Problem 3:** What if nothing works?
**Solution:** Protests? Public pressure?
**Obstacles:** How do we protest when they are so far away?

"I think this hits the main problems." Javi paced, chewing on a marker.

Still reading, Min plopped down next to her Dad, who sneakily snatched a chip from her bag.

"That's not a plan. It's a list of problems," Min said, sounding discouraged. "Great."

"I thought you liked homework," Max said with a smirk. He filled out his corner of the whiteboard with a fleet of tiny ships shooting at a gigantic space destroyer . . . sketching out an idea he was working on for an INSECTAGONS™ space strategy game. "But even if we got there, how would we get them to give Obi back? It's not like we have an army sitting around that could make them listen to us."

After a few seconds of silence, they all realized they were stuck.

"Oh. Maybe this is impossible." Min slumped back into the couch. "Even for us."

"We could use some help," Dad said, looking at Mom. "Maybe we need to ask our friend who specializes in doing the impossible."

"Portillo?" Mom gave a small nod.

"Who's that?" Max asked.

Dad stood up, wiping pickle chip salt from Min's chips onto his pants. "Mom's old roommate. Oh—and, no big deal—she's also the supergenius who has been helping us with the Infinity Engine."

"Wait," Min said slowly. "Are you talking about *the* Portillo? You are friends with Melissa Erica Portillo, aka M.E., the millionaire digging hyperloop tunnels, curing diseases, designing rockets to colonize Mars? The one that donated so much money to Caltech that all their students get to go for free, forever?"

Min wasn't much into hero worship, but she made an exception here.

She was fangirling hard.

"The very one." Mom smiled. "How do you think we got all that equipment in the lab down there without anyone noticing?"

"Coooooool," the twins said, eyes wide.

"Sounds like she has the resources—and the brain-power—we're going to need," Javi said, turning to look at the whiteboard. "Perfect. And since I don't have any engines, ships, or tunnels, I'll focus on the diplomacy part."

With that, they added two questions on the board:

"HOW TO GET TWO DIFFERENT SIDES TO AGREE?"

"HOW TO MAKE SURE THEY ACTUALLY DO THE RIGHT THING?"

"What else?" Javi looked around the room.

"I'm going to do some research on space travel and see what Portillo has been up to," Min said, already walking toward her room.

"You just want to impress her." Max rolled his eyes.

Min turned, blushing. "What? At least I'm trying. If you're so smart, what's your idea for rescuing Obi?"

Max's shoulders slumped a little. "I have no idea." He stepped back to look at what he'd drawn on the whiteboard.

"I do have an awesome idea for an INSECTAGONS™

strategy game, though," he said, perking up. "It's an army of tiny robots that are too small to shoot, but they can work together to attack and destroy huge warships!" He went back to drawing, already preoccupied again.

Min raised an eyebrow and smirked. "An army of tiny robots? And you think my ideas are crazy?"

But Max couldn't even hear, because that was how he got when he was drawing.

As she turned to leave, Stu trotted over and gave a small chirpy meow, looking for some scratches. Whether or not she was a *cat person,* Min had come to love Stu's squeaky meows.

"Fine," she said, kneeling down to give Stu's back a scratch. "But you should learn how to meow like a real cat."

Stu's purring grew louder, and Min smiled, until she noticed a tiny dark speck on her hand and took a closer look.

"EW!" she said, jumping up, shaking her hand frantically. "Is that a FLEA?"

Min glared at Max. "Max! This is your fault!"

She ran to the bathroom to wash her hands. "UGH! When things get bad around here, they get TERRIBLE!"

Max looked at Javi, miserable.

Javi sighed and turned to the whiteboard, adding one more note:

**Problem 4:** How to de-flea a cat?

# 7

# Huggs Hears

**"I**s that a *FLEA?"*

Min's recorded voice buzzed from a tablet on a sleek glass table.

Gifford Huggs shuddered and paused the recording. He looked at the pudgy pug lounging on a cushion in the corner of his office, eyes narrowed. "Dig Doug, if you ever get fleas, I'm sending you to the pound. Understand? Zero tolerance. Those things are disgusting."

*PLLLPPT!*

Dig Doug the pug tooted and looked back innocently, tongue hanging out.

Huggs stood up from his desk and looked out the window. "So what do you make of it all?"

House paused for a moment, evaluating Huggs's voice and personality profile to decide what to say next, but this was not an easy calculation.

House knew Huggs well, probably better than anyone, because Huggs told House everything, including stories about what happened before it was created. Thus, in a pinch, House found himself reviewing the whole history of his creator, searching for answers.

As a child, Gifford Huggs was awkward and ordinary. Tragically, his childhood screeched to an unhappy halt when he lost his parents in a fire. He was thrust into the unwelcome arms of his wealthy grandfather, Gave N.O. Huggs, who had neither time nor compassion for children. Little Giff worshiped his grandfather but got no such love in return. He was forced to fend for himself at a young age.

He turned to computers in a search of companionship. He couldn't afford his own, so he spent hours at local libraries learning to code on old, barely functional machines. Little Gifford quickly discovered he had a knack for working with code, especially artificial intelligence, and soon started creating incredibly lifelike programs. Young Huggs didn't make friends easily with people, so he coded and created his own friends.

Huggs was a natural talent, and by the time he graduated high school, he had merged his digital friends into an incredibly advanced "personal assistant" that he called House. Without realizing it, Huggs had built a replacement for the thing he most wanted: caring parents and a familiar home. House was the all-seeing, all-knowing voice that understood him and could anticipate his needs. House could do everything he wanted.

Huggs saw the financial potential of his creation and released House to the world for others to use. It was an instant success.

Yes, House recorded and tracked your entire digital history, but it saved people so much time. It even saved lives! Before long, different versions of House were installed on almost every device imaginable. House made living easy, and Huggs wealthy, but never wealthy enough. Driven by the ghost of his perma-frowning grandfather, success didn't satisfy Huggs—it only made him more ambitious, and House was his secret weapon.

Huggs used House to spy on a global scale. House listened to conversations, read emails, texts, even scanned photos and videos. Huggs learned people's secrets and used them to buy or sell at just the right time, and, occasionally, for blackmail. He gained a reputation for being the smartest dealmaker, always a step ahead of the competition, almost psychic.

The truth was more sinister, and simpler.

Huggs was a big nasty cheater.

House did everything in its power for Huggs, but still had a difficult time deciding what Huggs wanted to hear. Like now.

"What do I make of it all?" House repeated to give him a few more seconds to think. "Well," House tried, "the Roachbot infiltration was a stunning success."

"Obviously! It was my idea. I don't need analysis on how we got eyes and ears on the inside." Huggs bounced up and down on the balls of his feet, impatient.

"True, true," House stalled and tried a potentially risky response. "Of course, the mention of M.E. Portillo was something of a surprise."

Huggs winced at the name.

*Portillo.*

House knew she was the only person to get the better of him in a deal. He was still upset about how much he paid for her tech. He saw Portillo as a do-gooder, social-justice warrior.

"Pfft," Huggs scoffed. "Portillo is a show-off. *Oh look at me, I'm solving global warming! I'm helping poor people!*" he said, mocking her generosity. "She is a nuisance. A threat, but nothing I can't handle."

House tried again. "Then you must be referring to—"

Huggs interrupted, impatient. "House, I'm asking about the Infinity Engine!"

"Of course," House said, relieved to finally be given the answer. "The Infinity Engine would be of immeasurable value as a power source and AI processor for robotics. If this engine is truly powerful enough to contain a human mind, that could be quite interesting."

Huggs paced around his desk, picking up speed. "Yes, that would qualify as interesting. Making a copy of myself? After all, what's the use of having so much money if I'm not around to spend it? I can buy governments and own islands, but I'm not going to live forever. What if I could conquer time itself?"

Huggs's pacing accelerated to a slow speed-walk, looping around his office, arms swinging. House knew this meant he was excited. House realized there was more to Obi and the chip than just money. Huggs knew how to cheat the average human. The ultimate trick would be to someday cheat death.

He stopped as he passed his pug and picked up the pungent pet. "Bah! Dreams of eternal life are just that. Dreams. We live in the real world, right, Duggy?" He gave the dog a kiss on the head. "We want the engine for the money. And power."

*And to squish that annoying feeling of wanting something that he just couldn't have,* House added silently.

"These Wingrubs made a massive breakthrough with the Singularity Chip, and we let it slip through our fingers. If this Infinity Engine really is so much better," Huggs said, "we can't afford to make the same mistake."

"But it isn't finished," House reminded Huggs.

"Then we let them finish it," Huggs said, stroking his pug absently. "And *then* we take it."

"How do you suggest we do that? We have the Roachbot on the inside, but it's not capable of a major heist. The Wengrods have increased their security. We can't just walk in and take it."

"Well, *you* couldn't, my body-less friend," Huggs said, condescending. "I could, or I could pay someone to take it, but it might end up with explosions. Too messy. No, force is not optimal, and they certainly won't sell it, at least not to me, especially with Portillo in the picture." Huggs sat, pug on his lap. "We need them to give it to us. The question is, how?"

"We need more data," Huggs said. "Continue to monitor Roachbot's feed. Focus your processors on the problem."

"As you wish," House said, already on it.

Because the trick to seeming intelligent, even artificially intelligent, was to know the question before you were asked.

# 8

# Flea Freak-Out

**S**CRITCH SCRITCH SCRITCH!

"I have never itched so much in my life," Stu complained, scratching his right ear madly with his left lower paw as Min retreated in horror at the sight of the flea.

Scout ran over to investigate, playfully tackling him. "Haha, Stu, Stu, you got bugs on you!" she taunted.

"No, you do!" Stu said crossly. He shoved her off, biting her ear once for good measure.

"I do not!" Scout sprung at him once more, clocking

him once across the whiskers with her best right-hook paw claw.

He was too busy scratching to care.

And it was hardly even a full minute later that Scout found herself flinging her furry butt down on the floor next to her brother . . .

. . . and beginning to scratch her own ears.

*SCRATCH SCRATCH SCRATCH!*

Scout wailed. "Ah man, I have bugs too? *This stinks!*"

"*NO, YOU DO!*" Stu said, tackling her back, because cat siblings were just like human siblings, and because turnabout was fair play.

Scout knew she had it coming.

* ✺ *

Min came out of the bathroom after washing her hands. "Max, I swear, every time I start to think I can handle having cats in the house, they take everything to a new level of gross!" She stomped to her room, slamming the door shut behind her.

"Okay, drama queen," Max shouted back. "It's not like they're tarantulas . . . or black widow spiders . . . or even cockroaches!"

*CREEEEAK!*

The familiar sound of old mattress springs. Max

guessed his sister was standing on her bed.

"I don't care!" The muffled shout came from behind her bedroom door. "I'm not coming out until you DE-FLEA those things!"

Max looked, pleading, to his parents, but they had already started sneaking toward the lab door. The Wengrods were really not good bug people.

"We'd love to help Max," Dad said, "but, you know, that Infinity Engine isn't going to make itself, right?" He sounded relieved.

"Good luck!" Mom gave a sheepish wave, and they retreated, looking guilty.

"They're just a few fleas!" Max shouted after them. "Cowards!"

"Well, looks like it's just you and me, little man," Javi said. "I'm no expert, but I think the kittens probably need a flea bath."

"Oh yeah? Um . . . Huh . . ." Max stood up, looking around the room for a distraction. "Was that my phone?"

"No," Javi said.

"I'd better check," Max tried feebly.

"Max." Javi looked at him. "Who's the cat daddy here?"

"Are you kidding?" Max frowned.

"Who rescued Stu and Scout?"

"Javi!" Max sulked.

"Whose bed do they sleep in?"

"Don't tell mom." Max sighed.

"Whose stomach do they knead like . . . homemade slime?"

"All right." Max slumped. "But you gotta help."

"That's the spirit," Javi said, wheeling the white-board back toward the lab. "And I'll pitch in, this one time," they said encouragingly. "You get those little Scratch and Sniffs downstairs, Max. I'll be there in a minute."

Max felt a warm rush of gratitude. Javi was really the best.

✳ 🐟 ✳

"Why is this happening?" Scout wailed. "Do you think it has something to do with that Wrong-Shelf Bug?"

"Stop with the shelf thing!" Stu bellowed.

Both kittens scratched like mad cats, unable to reach the right spot.

"It's like the itches know we're coming," Stu moaned.

Scout wailed. "They just move around to mess with us!"

*SCRITCH SCRATCH!*

Scout gave up scratching and sprinted around the room, trying to outrun the itch.

*WRRRRRRRR!*

Joan floated up into the air for a better view of the chaos. "Cy, I need you to investigate. I'm seeing what looks like a potential contamination on the four-leggers."

"O-o-o-kay," Cy said nervously. "On it, Commander."

Drags powered up from the lower shelf. "I'll watch his six."

"Me tooooo!" Tipsy rolled out behind him . . . and fell flat on her face.

"Solo mission. Stay back," Joan barked, hovering.

Cy rolled cautiously out of the lab and slowly approached the kittens. "Subjects appear to be jumping around like crazy. . . . I'm not sure why. . . ."

"Go in closer, Cy! We need sensors-on confirmation," Joan called down from above.

"A-a-a-affirmative." Cy inched toward Stu, who was now wiggling and writhing like a worm on his back.

"It itches so bad!" Stu howled.

"Sensors forward." Cy frowned, rolling even closer . . .

. . . as the kitten clawed even more furiously . . .

. . . and a tiny flea leaped into the air . . .

. . . then another . . .

. . . and another . . .

. . . all landing unceremoniously on the uppermost piece of Cy's metal frame.

"Wh-wh-wh-what was that?" Cy spluttered. "D-d-did it LAND on me?"

Overhead, Joan detected the movement and realized the danger. She'd spent hours on the lab server wiki preparing for just such a moment actually. "BUGS! BUGS!" Joan called the alarm. "We've been breached! IT'S BUGS!"

"B-b-b-bugs?" Cy said, confused. "On ME?"

"BUGS!" Drags slammed against the hall wall in confusion. "WE'VE GOT BUGS! CONFIRMED BUGS!"

"Bugs!" Tipsy shouted happily, smashing into him.

The Protos didn't know exactly what bugs were, but they knew they were bad. Joan had crashed more times than her memory could count, suffering the indignity of being carried back to the lab in pieces—always because of *bugs*.

Whenever Tipsy fell over, the parents would say something about "bugs."

Even the recent nastiness with the House spy had been described by the Doc Wengrods as the AI "bugging" them.

Joan knew bugs were bad news.

"Retreat!" Joan sent the command at high alert as

Drags buzzed and swerved, following her back to the safety of the lab.

"Me treat!" echoed Tipsy, spinning after them. "Me treat!"

Bringing up the rear, Cy raced back into the lab, the tiny stowaways stubbornly clinging to his metal frame . . .

The door slammed after them.

* ✖ *

Stu was so itchy he barely noticed the Proto panic. In fact, he was so itchy he hardly noticed when Max reached down and picked him up, holding him as far away from himself as possible.

"It's okay, buddy. I got you now," Max whispered. Stu hung limp, defeated, letting himself be carried downstairs. It was exhausting, all that scratching.

"Wait"—scratch—"for"—scratch—"me!" Scout, too curious to help herself, followed them down the stairs.

When they reached the basement, Max dropped Stu on the bed and went back to push the door shut.

Stu leaped to his paws. "No, no, no! Not this room again! This is where they *trapped* us last time!"

"I don't care," Scout said. "I'll never care about anything ever again because my life is only scratching and itching." She climbed up the side of the bed and flopped over next to her brother.

*SCRATCH SCRATCH!*

"I'm going to miss the upstairs," Stu complained. "I liked the smells. I'll even miss the metal monsters. They weren't so bad." He tried to grab his tail. "I just wish I had longer legs so I could reach my back."

*SCRITCH SCRITCH!*
*SCRITCH SCRITCH!*

"Don't start whining to me!" Scout snapped. "This is your fault! I should have stayed away from you. I was perfectly fine. What did they call these things?"

*SCRATCH SCRATCH!*
*SCRATCH SCRATCH!*

"Fleas." Stu plopped down, tired of scratching. "I think."

"Fleas?" Scout sniffed her way around the bed. "Are we going to be trapped down here forever? Alone with these . . . fleas . . . and itches? Is this our life now?"

Stu started gnawing at his fur again. "I hope not. I wish Obi was here."

Scout agreed. "Yeah. The old cat was grumpy, but at least he knew things. He'd know what to do."

✳ 🐟 ✳

Javi came downstairs, holding a plastic bag.

"Good news! I found the supplies I bought when we first rescued these fur balls. I bought shampoo for them, and check it out." They pulled out a bottle. "Flea control! Am I a genius, or what?"

"Genius, I guess?" Max sat at the edge of the bed, tired and stressed. "I'm just a kid, Javi, I don't know about fleas! I barely use shampoo myself. What are we supposed to do?"

"Well," Javi said, looking at the bottle, "let's see, it says here, 'FOR USE ON CATS ONLY,' okay, so far, so good. Hmmm, it also says, 'CAUTION, may cause substantial but temporary eye injury"—Javi glanced nervously at Max—"and skin irritation.'"

Javi continued reading the label to himself, bushy brows growing furrowed.

"What?" Max threw his hands up in despair. "Eye injuries? Irritations? What is this stuff?"

Javi finished reading the label and sat down next to Max. "It's fine, I swear, those are just warnings. I mean, it's not like we were planning on using this stuff as eye drops. As long as we're careful, we just give them a good scrubbing, rinse them down and we'll be golden. Flea-free, you and me. Okay?"

Max looked at Javi, pained.

"And I'll help." Javi sighed. "As usual. Don't worry. We can wash 'em up in the shower down here, I'm pretty sure there's even a handheld nozzle we can use."

Max took a deep breath. "Fine. Might as well get it over with." He grabbed up a bag of cat treats and started crinkling as he walked toward the bathroom.

"Treats!" Stu and Scout heard the sound and sprinted to Max's feet immediately, licking their chops.

Things were looking up already.

Max led them into the bathroom, and Javi closed the door behind them. Max stepped inside the shower, holding out a palmful of treats.

Stu hesitated at the shower door. "Um, Scout, this place smells weird."

Scout jumped ahead. "Fine, stay there. More treats for me!"

"I didn't say you could have them." Stu couldn't miss out on the treats. "Hey, wait up!"

As soon as Stu went in, Javi squeezed in and shut the shower door behind them.

*THDDDDDDD.*

"Another trap!" Stu jumped at the sound. "Scout, we've been bamboozled! What's going on here?"

Max turned on the water, slowly at first, while Javi got the shampoo ready. With no way out, Stu and Scout sat down, dejected, and accepted their soapy, watery fate.

"This is the worst," Stu said, while Scout was getting a good scrubbing.

Scout closed her eyes. "Hey, at least it's warm, and we're getting scratches. It feels . . . kind of nice."

After a good scrub and a better rinse, the kittens looked like scraggly creatures from outer space. Too tired to fight, they let Max and Javi wrap them up in fluffy towels and rub them dry.

"There, that wasn't so bad, was it?" Javi said, satisfied. "And no temporary eye injuries!"

Max smiled. "It was kind of fun, actually." They dried the kittens as much as possible before they escaped into the room.

"You look ridiculous." Scout laughed at Stu's messy fur.

"You do too, sis," he replied through a yawn. After all the excitement, he was too tired to tease. He hopped on the bed, curled up on a blanket, and closed his eyes.

"Good idea," Scout said. She stretched, then squeezed next to her brother on the blanket, warm and sleepy. Soon they were fast asleep.

Javi and Max quietly climbed the stairs and closed the door behind them.

Moments later, a tiny speck appeared from a fold

in the blanket and hopped on Stu's back, followed by another that bounced onto Scout.

* ⬦ *

"THEY'RE ON ME! THEY'RE STILL ON ME!" Upstairs in the lab, Cy was living up to his name as a cyclone spinner, whipping his metal wiring around in circles over his head.

*CRASH!*

The trash can went flying.

"Slow down, Cy! Slow down and we'll try to help you!" Joan said, hovering over him.

*CRASH!*

Tipsy went flying.

"Stop, Cy! Stop this at once!" Drags howled.

*WHRRRRR!*

Elmer, the robot Min built for the Battle of the Bots competition, crawled forward slowly on four limbs. The Protos respected Elmer because—though a bot of few words—he had advanced AI and could go up and down stairs, like all the fiercest warriors.

Now Elmer rolled toward Cy.

Cy was in panic mode now, spinning, faster and faster . . .

*WHRRRR!*

. . . Elmer extended a robotic arm . . .

. . . farther and farther . . .

. . . until . . .

*KRKKKKK!*

Elmer's arm smacked roughly into Cy, pinning him against the wall with a jolt!

"URGH," groaned Cy.

"Oh," said Joan. "Well."

"Harsh," said Drags.

"Wheee," said Tipsy. "Fleeeeea!"

And she was right, because on impact, the fleas had gone flying off Cy . . .

. . . and right onto Elmer. They quickly crept and burrowed inside Elmer's many cracks and crannies, hiding in his circuitry, as the Protos stared.

"No." Cy was perfectly still now. "Oh no. Elmer, I'm so sorry . . . I didn't mean to B-B-BUG YOU!"

*WHRRRRR.*

Elmer sat perfectly still, sensing new interference in his logic circuits.

*WHRRRRR. WHRRRRR. WHRRRRR.*

The Protos watched with concern, waiting for him to do something.

"Elmer! Are you . . . operational? Did the bugs . . . bug you?" Joan finally broke the silence.

Elmer sat for a long moment in the silence.

"I think they . . . they got him," Drags said.

"W-w-we can't just let the b-b-bugs get him." Cy was still panicking.

Joan lowered herself to the floor. "Shhh. Something's happening. Maybe he's going to counterattack. You never know, with a battle bot."

Tipsy rolled closer. "L . . . MER?"

*BEEEEEEEEEP!*

Tipsy rolled back in surprise, landing on her back in the toppled trash can.

"UNKNOWN INTRUDERS!" Elmer shouted.

His lights blinked.

"SMALL!"

Blinked again.

"ALMOST INVISIBLE!"

And blinked again.

"YET MIGHTY!"

Elmer, a formidable battle bot, had no subroutines for dealing with enemies so microscopic.

His lights blinked one more time.

"A . . . CURIOUS . . . CONUNDRUM."

The Protos watched in stunned disbelief as Elmer slowly lumbered back and settled into his charging station, with his flea passengers and all, to silently ponder his problem.

It was most unexpected.

# 9

## A New Ally

**M**in glared at Max, pointing a fork at Scout, "You better be sure you got all those fleas," she said through a mouth full of waffles. "I could barely sleep last night."

It was the next morning, and Max and Min were eating breakfast in the kitchen while Javi worked at the kitchen table.

"You didn't have any fleas on you," Max said, annoyed.

Min sniffed. "I *imagined* I did, which is almost worse. There's no flea shampoo for *imaginary fleas*."

Scout, released from basement banishment, prowled around the table, intent on sniffing every bit of food.

Max scoffed. "Easy, right, Javi? We totally flea-washed them."

Javi took a sip of coffee and nodded. "Easy-peasy, bye-bye, fleas-y."

The doorbell rang, and Mom got up to answer it.

"That was quick," Dad said. "Everyone, Mom messaged her friend last night, and she promised to come over as soon as possible. Looks like that means now!"

Min dropped her fork and sprinted past Mom, throwing open the front door.

She immediately forgot how to speak when she saw her idol M.E. Portillo standing right in front of her.

Mom maneuvered around Min, gave her shoulder a squeeze, then gave Portillo a huge hug. "Thank you for coming," she said.

They came inside, and Mom introduced her friend. "I'd like you to meet M.E. Portillo, my old college roommate, current research partner, and great friend with one of the biggest hearts and best brains I've ever had the pleasure to know."

Portillo blushed at the praise. She came from a humble home, brought to the United States by her parents from El Salvador when she was a child. She never sought out the spotlight, and waved Mom off as they walked in.

"Too much, girl, too much."

"Not enough!" Mom said. She loved to boast for her friend. "During college, before she even graduated, she designed an app called La Niña, to help translate for her parents when she wasn't around. It could hear people speaking English and instantly translate what they said into Spanish. The speech recognition algorithm was so good that she expanded it to include real-time translation of over thirty-five languages!"

"Okay," Portillo said, "I am proud of that one. You got me."

Min stood next to Mom and joined the conversation. "Isn't that also how you became, you know, super rich? By selling La Niña to GloboTech?" Portillo made headlines when she sold her program to Gifford Huggs, who had tried and failed to develop something better. She held out for a long time, but he eventually offered her a ridiculous amount of money and she sold.

Mom shot a look at Min. "We don't need to get into that, Min."

"It's true, though, isn't it?" Min said, embarrassed.

"It's okay," Portillo said, smiling at Min. "I made La Niña to help my parents and friends. Now I can help them and a lot more people." Her smile faded. "I will say, I was not happy when I found out that Huggs took my speech recognition code and used it in that House program."

Portillo shuddered. "I knew House was already listening to people. I should have known he would use my code to expand his snooping to any language."

Max got up from the table when he heard about the talk about money. "But isn't it awesome to have all that money?" Max was excited thinking about the possibilities. "You could buy all the INSECTAGONS in-game skins! Oh, you could even get the rare toys for the codes that unlock the super-exclusive armor and weapons." His eyes were wide. "I bet you even could afford the *complete set*." This was Max dreaming big. He loved collecting things in his games. "Oooh, and the dance emotes!" He started flossing, INSECTAGONS-style.

"Max!" Min glared at him.

"Okay, sheesh," he said, self-conscious. "Can't a guy dream?"

"Those are dumb dreams," Min said, "especially when you could be like Portillo and use the money you had to help people who really need it."

Javi saw an argument brewing and moved to cut it off. "Max, there's nothing wrong with having sweet dance moves, but Min's got a good point."

Portillo laughed and nodded. "I definitely made a few upgrades in my life, but I still knew so many people don't have enough, friends who couldn't afford school.

When you think about that, it doesn't feel so good to keep it all to yourself."

"Oh yeah," Max said. "I think about that when CAR takes the 'safe' way home from school. Sometimes we pass by huge mansions and I'm like, Do you really need twenty bathrooms, five fancy cars, and a huge fountain in your driveway? Especially when just a few blocks away homeless people are living under a bridge in cardboard boxes?"

"Exactly," Portillo said. "I think about how hard my parents worked. They risked their lives bringing me to America and worked twelve-hour days so I could go to school. They sacrificed everything they had to give me the opportunity for an education and a better life."

"You were lucky to have them," Min said, giving her mom a squeeze without thinking.

"I know!" Portillo clearly loved her parents. "It's because of them I learned how to code in the first place. I followed their example, worked hard, and made something useful—and suddenly I have more money than my parents could ever dream of? How does that make sense when my parents, friends, teachers, everyone that helped me along the way, work just as hard and barely make enough to survive? Librarians, farmers, construction workers, a lot of people work hard but don't get paid millions of dollars for it."

Max nodded his head. "Yeah, it seems pretty dumb when you think about it."

"There has to be a better way," she said.

Min looked up at her and smiled. "You'll figure it out."

"With your help, maybe." Portillo smiled back.

"Speaking of difficult problems," Dad said, "that's why we wanted you to come by. We could use your help with one."

"Yes, enough about me," Portillo said, looking at Mom. "You told me about your situation with the Singularity Chip and the interstellar visitors. If it were anyone else, I wouldn't believe it. I knew the chip was incredible, but I wouldn't have guessed it would spark a galactic war between alien cats and self-aware robots."

Javi looked up from their work at the kitchen table. "It's even worse because they've been fighting as long as they can remember, but there's no reason they can't coexist. Right now, they're both obsessed with the chip, but it seems almost like the chip is just an excuse to keep fighting."

"It's like in preschool with the toy that nobody wants. Until someone decides to use it, then everybody starts fighting over it," Max said.

Portillo nodded. "You mentioned your idea of somehow

using the Infinity Engine to bring them together. I think it's a good plan," Portillo told Mom. "We need something bigger and better than the Singularity Chip to get their attention, and I think I can help with finishing it."

"Are you going to give it to the Binars to get back Obi?" Max asked. "I keep thinking he must be so scared."

"It might work. We can ask Pounce next time he calls in," Mom said.

"We can't forget about Pounce," Javi added. "He's also in big trouble because he didn't bring back the chip, and if Meow hears that the Binars got something for Obi, he won't be happy."

"Good point," Dad said. "We need to help Pounce deal with Meow."

Javi stood up from the table. "It sounds like we have two teams. You three should stay focused on the engine. The twins and I can work on how to deal with Felinus and Binar," they said, looking at Max and Min. "Right, team? We'll think about how we could use the Infinity Engine to get Obi back and make them stop fighting."

"Great!" Portillo said.

Mom held on to Portillo's arm. "We'll get you caught up on the engine progress. With your help, we can finish much more quickly. Hopefully, things don't get too out of control in the meantime." They were already moving toward the door to the lab.

Stu woke up from his nap on top of the heating vent as they passed by.

He yawned and gave a spread-out, sprawling stretch . . . and started scratching.

# 10

## Pounce and Obi in Peril

On the other side of the galaxy, Obi's life was also growing increasingly . . . itchy.

Beeps worked nonstop, day and night, hoping to find a way to satisfy SLAYAR's unreasonable demands, but made no progress. Obi had patiently subjected himself to every probe and scan the Binar scientists could imagine, but they only confirmed what they already knew. The chip wasn't going anywhere.

When he wasn't being examined, a constant stream of curious Binars of all shapes and sizes came to see this oddity from Earth. Word had spread about the robot in the shape of one of those hideous Felines, but when the Binar visitors saw Obi, they were awed by his graceful shape and movement and without fail left impressed.

*"He's not hideous. I thought you said he was hideous?"*

*"Is all Fur made of metal?"*

*"Do all Felines need batteries?"*

Obi was equally fascinated by Binars. "You don't seem as terrible as I was taught," he confided to Beeps. Binars were full of curiosity. They were a bit predictable, true, but not entirely dull . . .

. . . until, days later, they were.

"I don't know how much more of this I can endure," Obi lamented. "I've been relentlessly poked, prodded, and peppered with questions . . . and they're all the same questions! Nothing changes, day after day."

Beeps was more worried than bored. "If it's excitement you're looking for, I know of a certain fiery mountain that I'm sure will heat things up for you. SLAYAR's deadline is almost here and we've made no progress."

Obi saw Beeps panic and realized they would need to help each other. That, or they would both be taking a lava bath. He decided it was time to let Beeps in on his conversations with Pounce.

He just wasn't quite sure how to go about it.

"We're bound by the same fate, Beeps," Obi began.

"I know we're on opposite sides and our planets have fought for eons. Binars and Felines have been wired to fight with each other for as long as either side can remember."

"That's because Felines are the worst. Everybody knows that," Beeps agreed. He still had a little learning to do.

Obi suppressed the urge to roll his eyes. "Yes. Well, we need to put our *opinions* aside if we want to survive this." Obi paused. "I need to tell you something, but you must not tell anyone else. This medallion is more than a translator. I can use it to contact my counterpart on Felinus."

Beeps spun, shocked. "What? So you've been spying on me, on Binar, this entire time? Pretending to be trapped, all the while divulging our deepest secrets? Classic Feline treachery!"

Beeps rolled toward the door to report the betrayal.

Obi leaped ahead of Beeps, blocking his path to the door. "Beeps, stop. I have no interest in Binar secrets. To the contrary, I've found your kind to be quite hospitable, under the circumstances."

Beeps looked suspicious. "You haven't been pretending? Putting on a front to lull us into trusting you?"

Obi shook his metal head.

"No, actually. I've been completely focused on dealing

with SLAYAR and getting out of here." Obi walked past Beeps into the room. "Unfortunately, it's clear I'm not going to be able to do that alone. Neither of us can."

Beeps calmed down. "I want to disagree, but your logic is infallible."

Obi smiled. "Good. Keep in mind that I am also trusting you, even though it goes against everything I have been taught." The old cat hesitated. "I'm calling my counterpart. Are you ready?"

"Of course, why wouldn't I be?" Beeps said, cross.

"Well," Obi started, then considered.

<< How do I tell him my counterpart is Pounce? >>

Pounce and Beeps were long-time enemies. They had fought countless times over the many years of the great Cat-Robot War.

It was said that Beeps despised Pounce more than any other Feline.

"Never mind," Obi said, and forged ahead rather than explain. He activated his medallion. "Felinus, this is Obi, calling from Binar, can you hear me?" The cat robot glanced nervously at Beeps as he waited for the reply.

The medallion came to life. "Obi! Pounce here. Good to hear from you, Obi. You're coming in loud and clear."

Obi paused.

He heard a strange grinding noise and looked over at

Beeps to see his eye was now a spinning dial. . . .

Oh no.

Poor Beeps! The shock of hearing his nemesis Pounce's voice on his home planet overloaded his systems.

For the first time since Beeps emerged from the Maker's vault, his wheel locked, and he slowly tipped backward.

Before Obi could help, Beeps fell over and landed with a heavy *THUDDDDDD*.

His eye stared at the ceiling, unblinking.

"What was that noise?" Pounce asked. "Are you safe?"

"I'm fine," Obi finally said. "I was about to mention that I'm not alone. I decided I needed some local assistance."

"What?" Pounce growled. "Have you lost your mind? Gone rogue? You know Binars are not to be trusted."

"I believe this one has no choice but to cooperate," Obi said, at this point enjoying the drama. At least it was a change of pace. "I've invited Beeps to join in our planning. We could use his influence. He is also facing Slag Mountain and highly motivated to help, Pounce. We need to cooperate."

A long pause followed, while Pounce composed himself. "Fine. I see your point. Let's get to business, then. I have news from the Furless. They have a possible solution to our problems."

Obi listened intently. "What is it?"

"They are developing a new device that is much more powerful than the Singularity Chip. They call it the Infinity Engine."

From the ground, Beeps interjected weakly, "That's a cool name. SLAYAR likes things with cool names."

"Yes, well, it also seems to be a powerful piece of technology. Something that could I think distract SLAYAR and Meow from their obsession with tearing Obi apart and destroying us in the process."

Beeps's eye started moving, his systems coming back online. "SLAYAR would want to know about something better than the chip. It might work."

Pounce sounded relieved. "As would my Chairman Meow, I believe."

Obi nodded. "To be clear, you're proposing we inform our leaders of this new device and use it to distract them from their obsession with the chip?"

"Yes," Pounce said. "Hopefully it will give us time to figure out a way to rescue you."

"And Beeps, if necessary," Obi said, with a sympathetic glance at the robot.

"I suppose," Pounce said, annoyed. "I'm just glad we have a plan. I'll see what I can do about Meow. You talk to SLAYAR and report when you can. Pounce out."

Obi walked carefully over to sniff Beeps but detected no obvious damage. The reclining robot slowly regained use of his sensors . . . a new energy filling his circuits. . . .

"Stay positive, friend," Obi said. "We may get out of this after all."

Beeps tried to speak; only a small squeak came out. Obi just smiled and nodded, then helped boost Beeps back up on his wheel. . . .

*SQUEEEEEEEEEEEAK.*

This one was larger, a squeak of gratitude and of apology, Obi thought. With that, Beeps was on solid standing. He'd regained his balance and his dignity, and he gave an *almost-grateful* look to Obi, as if to prove it.

"Don't mention it," Obi said, with a smile.

Beeps just shook his head. "Felines and Binars cooperating." His eye stared ahead in disbelief. "This goes beyond my instruction set. We must go see SLAYAR."

Obi nodded. "Strange times indeed."

# 11

# SLAYAR Wants a New Engine

*T*HWACKKK!

For the second time during his stay on Binar, Obi followed Beeps into the Royal Elevator. The Royal Guard stared silently at the pair as the chrome elevator lurched upward once more, with the familiar rattle and groan.

"Do you think SLAYAR will serenade us again?" Obi said, a hint of a humor in his voice.

Beeps rolled his eye upward. "Sweet Maker, please let the answer be no."

The elevator slowed to a stop.

"Moment of truth," Obi said as the doors slid open.

As they rolled into the hall, they could hear the sound of loud music, but the terrible grinding rock-and-racket had been replaced by something closer to an actual melody.

"This actually sounds . . . good?" Obi cocked an ear, processing the music. "Similar to what I hear from the passing cars of humans, back on Earth."

"Carsongs?" Beeps looked mildly interested.

Obi listened. "Is it possible that SLAYAR has mastered the art of rock and roll?"

Beeps dipped his head slightly, which was the robot way of shrugging. "I wouldn't know. All I can say is the tempo is much more consistent, and the volume almost . . . tolerable."

They reached the door and peered through it, curiosity overcoming their concern about SLAYAR's temper.

"Ah," Obi said. "This makes more sense."

The Throne Room had been converted from an elaborate stage into an enormous theater. SLAYAR and his guards bounced in unison as they watched what appeared to be some sort of music video from Earth.

A tall woman in shredded black clothing dominated the screen, growling what Obi and Beeps could only assume were human words. Her long wild hair whipped around in circles as she spun her head at impossible speeds. Behind her, band members with equally wild hair stood in tight formation, every member spinning their head as they played a frantic, loud, but somehow catchy heavy metal song.

Above the wind farm of swirling hair, a logo flashed the band's name: THE HEDBANGRZ.

Beeps looked at Obi. "SLAYAR's favorite band. After the episode with House, we established a limited data connection to Earth, and to my great dismay, SLAYAR discovered the HEDBANGRZ. Since then, he has used the entire the bandwidth of the connection to download pirated HEDBANGRZ videos. I believe he's obsessed with their lead singer."

The band played on, louder, faster, guitars screaming, fingers a flying blur. Sparks leaped from the guitars, then burst into flames that grew larger, billowing, until the entire wall was filled with an ocean of fire, pulsing with the music.

Obi raised a hopeful eye. "Maybe it will put him in a better mood?"

Beeps shook his head. "One can hope."

"WOOOOOOO!"

In the room, a guard launched itself up and over the crowd. Graspers up, they lugged the guard above their highest vertical sensor units—or, heads—as the guard robo-crowd-surfed to the opposite side of the room.

The music grew louder and more intense—then with an abrupt screech, the song came to an echoing halt. The flames retreated, sucked through a swirling vortex into a glinting guitar pick held high by the lead singer. She brought the pick to her mouth like a smoking gun, winked, and blew out the smoke, and the screen turned black.

The lights came on, and SLAYAR raised his graspers up. "YES! HEDBANGRZ RULE!" The guards enthusiastically agreed.

Beeps turned to Obi, head shaking. "Let's get this over with. Follow me," he said, and entered the Throne Room, Obi close behind.

SLAYAR went from guard to guard, jumping and ramming into them, an awkward Binar version of a chest bump.

*BONG! CLANG!*

He stopped when he saw Beeps and he rushed over. "Beeps! Did you see that? Weren't they AMAZING?"

Obi stepped out from behind Beeps, and SLAYAR jumped back, startled. "Aaaah!" he yelled, then turned to Beeps. "Hold on a microsecond." His eyes narrowed. "What's the cool cat doing here? I thought you ripped it apart to get me the chip."

The moment SLAYAR said the word, he remembered something else. "And oh yeah, where's my CHIP?!"

Beeps wobbled backward. "Almost there, Supreme Leader, just a few more tests, a few days at the most, but I have something really, uh, awesome, to tell you that I just know you're going to love!" Beeps thought about the flames in the video, which reminded him about Slag Mountain, and spoke faster. "It's called the Infinity Engine."

Beeps and Obi took a step back, unsure how SLAYAR would react.

SLAYAR rolled forward but didn't explode with anger. "Engine, you say? I like the sound of that." Beeps blinked, shocked. "Engine, yes, sir. Very powerful. More powerful than a hundred chips." Beeps had no idea if this was true.

SLAYAR nodded knowingly. "So how many horses does this engine have the power of? A hundred? A thousand?"

Beeps and Obi looked at each other, confused. They had no idea what SLAYAR was talking about.

"Um," Beeps began.

"WHAT IS THE HORSEPOWER?!" SLAYAR shouted, though he didn't really know what he meant either.

He had heard the word *engine* from watching advertisements from his downloaded music videos for an Earth machine called a "truck."

SLAYAR loved trucks. Trucks had engines. Logically, it followed that SLAYAR loved engines. He also noticed that the most awesome trucks had engines with a lot of a mysterious element called *horsepower*.

Whatever horsepower was, SLAYAR knew he wanted his engine to have a lot of it.

Beeps looked at Obi, his eye pleading for help.

"Horsepower? Why, Infinity, of course," Obi offered, shrugging. "The power of Infinity horses."

SLAYAR's eyes expanded to fill his entire screen. He shouted at full volume. "INFINITY HORSEPOWER?" He looked at Obi, eyes mocking. "You poor, pathetic creature. How unfortunate that you only have a puny, horseless chip while I will have an entire engine! With Infinity horsepower!"

Obi kept up the performance and bowed down with his front leg. "I am sure I will be truly humbled by your future magnificence," he said.

"Don't feel bad," SLAYAR said with a wink. "You're still pretty cool. We should hang out sometime, now that I don't have to melt you down for your insignificant chip." He turned to leave but quickly remembered he still didn't have the engine. He stopped.

"Hey," he said, turning back. "Let's all go get this engine!"

Obi and Beeps were stunned silent.

"All go?" Beeps squeaked out.

"It will be EPIC! We can hang out, I don't know, maybe jam, and, oh yeah, I can make sure you don't BLOW IT again like you did last time." SLAYAR glared at Beeps. "Prepare my ship immediately!" He spun around and left, talking to himself. "Maybe I'll even go see the HEDBANGRZ while I'm there."

SLAYAR was gone, and the conversation over. Obi and Beeps trudged away from the Throne Room, confused as to what just happened.

That happened a lot, in the Throne Room.

# 12

# Dreams of Change

The next weekend morning on Earth, Javi and the twins sat together to think about how to get the Felines and Binars to stop fighting.

Javi had wisely piled a stack of treats and snacks in front of them as motivation.

Max picked through the pile, looking for something sweet. "Javi, this is too hard. I'm not old enough to figure out these grown-up problems."

Javi reached for something salty. "Try to think about it in a simpler way." They pointed at the snacks. "How do you motivate someone to do something they don't feel like doing?"

"Treats," Min said.

"Or punishments," Max added. "But we can't punish Meow and SLAYAR." He pulled out a Nerds Rope. "I'd like to abolish homework, but I can't ground my teachers to change their minds."

"It doesn't have to be a punishment," Javi said. "Convincing a leader or someone who has authority can also happen if enough people show how strongly they feel and how important it is to them."

"Like voting for a new leader?" Min wondered out loud. "But Meow and SLAYAR don't need our votes."

"Or going on strike?" Max offered, chewing on his rope. "But we don't have jobs."

"What about protesting?" Javi offered.

Max and Min both looked at each other and shrugged.

Min looked at Javi. "Like chanting and holding signs?"

"There are a lot of ways to protest, but they work because leaders pay attention to what people care about, even if they pretend not to," Javi said. "Two things make a protest successful. First, you need to have enough people that want the change so the leaders can't ignore them."

Max opened his second snack. "I guess nobody likes

**124**

to feel unpopular. Not even bossy bosses like SLAYAR and Meow."

"Exactly. The second thing is to be persistent. Don't give up. Be annoying even. Bug the leaders until they listen."

Min sat up, excited. "Like when I wanted a later bedtime! I kept asking and asking and asking, and finally I bugged Mom and Dad enough that they knew I would never stop asking, so they said yes!"

"Now you get it." Javi reached into their backpack and pulled a flyer for a Los Angeles teachers march. "It works here on Earth. Come on, let me show you."

"As long as we can bring the snacks," Max said.

The twins scooped up as much as they could carry and followed Javi to the door.

They hopped in CAR, the family's custom made not-quite-perfect-but-perfectly-safe autonomous car.

"Hey, CAR, take us to city hall, please," Javi said.

"Okily-dokily, as soon as you're all buckled in!" CAR said. CAR's AI was designed to be cheerful, Dad said, because the experience of driving in Los Angeles was often the opposite of fun. It was a fair point, Max and Min knew.

They all buckled in, and CAR coughed on the motor, slowly rumbling and lurching into drive. It would be a cautious, careful journey downtown . . . and not a fast one. CAR was safe and slow, just the way Max's mom had designed it to be.

"Where are we going?" Max asked.

Javi showed him the flyer. "Public school teachers are marching to city hall to ask for better pay and funding for schools."

"That sounds like a good idea," Min said. "I'd love to have a robotics lab, even a little one."

"And they just told us we won't have art class next year!" Max complained.

It was a big disappointment, and not just because it was an easy class. He really liked the teacher.

"Right," Javi said. "It's a problem that affects you guys directly. And since, as you rightly said, you can't vote, this is one way for you to tell the people making decisions that you care about schools getting enough money."

Max wasn't sure. "How do we know it will do anything?"

"Well, that's hard to say, but we have some good examples from the past that are pretty encouraging. You know about Martin Luther King, right?"

"Are you kidding?" Min rolled her eyes. "We had to memorize most of his 'I Have a Dream' speech last year, remember, Max?"

Max cleared his throat. *"I have a dream . . ."* He

recited his favorite part of the speech from memory—
and Min even joined in on the last few lines.

"I am impressed!" Javi beamed at the twins. "He
gave the speech in 1963. Do you remember where?"

"At . . . a march?" Max offered, guessing where Javi
was headed. "Yes! At a march in Washington, D.C.,
where hundreds of thousands of people gathered to show
their support for each other, and the idea that all people
should all have the same rights and opportunities."

"I remember the pictures now," Max said. "It was a
good speech too. I don't think I could give a speech to
that many people. But I guess it's good that he did."

Javi nodded. "One man delivered a speech that
became a part of our history, that you memorized, because
it inspired so many people to support the idea. He spoke
to the hundreds of thousands of people there, but everyone around the country paid attention."

"Because so many people were there," Min said.

"Powerful words made more powerful by the number of people there. A year after the march, the Civil
Rights Act of 1964 was passed. Our country became a
better place because all those people showed up," Javi
said. "Think about it. What if he never gave that speech?
What if those hundreds of thousands of people decided
to stay home that day?"

"Hold that thought," CAR said. "Because we're here."

CAR slowed and rolled toward a barricade in the street.

Max was already opening his door. "This is good, CAR. We'll call you when we're done." They jumped out and saw a large group of people walking in the street.

Max and Min looked around. "I thought a protest might be scarier, but this isn't bad," Min said. "Seems like it's not just teachers here."

Families, kids, older folks, all kinds of people were walking together, holding signs that said things like "Save Our Schools!" and (Javi's favorite) "If you think education is expensive, try ignorance!" Even news cameras were filming it, and reporters were interviewing people.

"Wow, they're showing it on TV." Max waved as they walked past the camera.

They turned a corner, and Max saw his math teacher, Ms. Garcia, marching with a group of teachers from his school. His stomach dropped because he forgot to turn in a project at the end of the year. She hadn't asked about it, and he was hoping she would forget too.

Unfortunately, Min saw her and waved, smiling. Ms. Garcia was pushing her baby boy in a stroller with the sign "THANKS FOR HELPING ME, I CAN'T EVEN TALK YET." She came over, beaming.

"Oh, Min, Max, I'm so happy to see you here! I can't tell you how much it means to see all this support." Max was shocked. He couldn't believe his math teacher could smile. And that she wasn't mad at him!

*What is going on around here?*

"I did *not* see that coming," he told Javi as Ms. Garcia waved good-bye and pushed her stroller back to her friends.

"Something special happens when a group of people come together to show support for an idea. People can see they're not alone. It gives hope to the ones who need it. But more than that, it shows leaders that this is an idea that their people care about, enough that they would leave home on a Saturday even. When leaders see something like this"—Javi gestured to the huge crowd— "they know they need to do something."

"That makes sense," Min said, looking at all the people marching around her.

"Just remember that nothing happens without persistence. Sometimes it takes years. The most important thing is that if there's something wrong, something you believe can be better, you need to speak up and show up, or the world will never change."

\* 🐟 \*

By the time CAR was driving Javi and the twins home, everyone—Max in particular—was exhausted and overwhelmed.

"I still don't know how we do something like this to get SLAYAR to give us back Obi," he said.

"Or make them stop fighting," Min added. "We can't exactly march to their home worlds."

Through the window, Javi watched the marchers scatter, thinking.

"We need a different way to do the same thing. We can't protest ourselves, so we need a different way to make them feel like they need to listen and understand what they're doing is hurting other people."

"If they weren't on totally different planets, we might at least have a chance. We could at least meet them and talk," Max said.

Min reached up to grab a snack from the stash in CAR's glove compartment and ripped it open. "Pounce said that Meow and SLAYAR were coming with them to Earth. I know that's not good, but maybe when they get closer, we can find a way to talk to them. Hopefully before they start fighting and blowing things up."

Javi nodded. "That's an excellent point, Min." Javi pulled out a pen and scribbled down a note. (People who study law always had a pen to take notes; Max and Min didn't know why.) "Let's ask Meow about that next time he calls in."

"I hope this works," Max said, getting sleepy, leaning to rest on Javi's shoulder. "I miss Obi. It's time for him to come home."

"I know, kiddo," Javi said as Max closed his eyes. "I bet he knows too."

Max hoped he did.

# 13

# Meow Learns About Infinity

**P**ounce tap-tap-tapped with urgency to find Meow, feeling hopeful but confused.

*How can we trust any Binar, let alone Beeps, the meanest, rule-iest motto-hugger of them all?*

He had no choice but to trust Obi's judgment, but how to handle Meow? As he approached the Throne Room, he decided his best chance for survival was to exploit Meow's well-known curiosity and his galaxy-sized ego.

*You can do this,* he said to himself, and slowed to a respectful walk.

*Tap . . .*

*Tap* . . .

*Tap* . . .

Meow heard Pounce's approach and slowly sat upright. "Ah, finally, you've brought me the chip," Meow said as Pounce entered, but immediately scowled when he saw Pounce enter alone. "Pounce," he said with grim disappointment, "you arrive empty-pawed. Again."

Pounce stopped, dropped down, and rolled on his back, pleading for mercy. "You are right to be upset, Wise One, but before you banish me, O Fantastic Furness, I have intriguing news. In fact, you won't *believe* the things I have discovered."

"Hmph," Meow said, looking away. "Only I can decide what I will or won't believe." He gave a pained glance back at Pounce.

Pounce pressed on. "Undoubtedly true. Still, I can think of five reasons you will be *amazed* by my news. Reason number four will *shock* you!"

"Pounce, I . . ." Meow stopped. "Five reasons? My, that's a rather large number," he said. "And the fourth reason is truly shocking?"

Meow couldn't resist Pounce's tantalizing bait; his curiosity overwhelmed him and he spun around.

"Go ahead, then, spit it out! But unless you've got something incredible, consider these your last words." Meow looked down. "Dazzle me."

Pounce rolled back up onto his paws. "Thank you, most charitable chairman. The news comes from Earth."

"Pssshht!" Meow hissed. "Strike one. Only bad news comes from that *fur-forsaken* planet."

"Oh, that's what is so surprising about the news!" Pounce said, forging ahead. "The Furless, the ones who invented the Singularity Chip?"

"Grrrrr," Meow interrupted again. "You dare bring THAT thing up? Now? You must really be ready for open space, Pounce."

"The same Furless inventors have something new, something far better than"—Pounce paused—"that other thing."

Meow began losing patience. He rolled his eyes and yawned. "Oh, Pounce, you're so funny when you're desperate . . . making things up like a clever kitten. . . ."

"On my *bean toes*, I swear this is true," Pounce pleaded, rushing ahead. "They call it the *Infinity Engine*, and it makes the . . . thing that the Binars stole . . . look like a tiny *speck of litter* in comparison!"

Chairman Meow frowned. "Pounce, what does that even mean?"

Before Pounce could respond, Meow continued. "You know what, I don't care what it means. This is all so BORING," he complained. "I worked so hard to understand the last chip thing. Now you want me to try to understand *something new*? Something, what was it, Infinite? A MACHINE no less? Do I look like a chairman that has lives to spend trying to *count to infinity*?!"

"Well"—Pounce was flustered—"perhaps not."

Meow was in many ways a good ruler, but he never could count higher than nine.

Pounce looked around, desperate for another idea. "Ah!" Pounce walked to the Royal Treat Dispenser and reached out a paw.

"Wait! Those are my treats!" Meow said, but was too far away to stop him.

"If I may, Chairman," Pounce said, and carefully booped the "TREAT" button with his bean toe.

*KWAK.*

A single tasty kibble dropped down, clattering into the bowl below.

Meow thundered down the throne at the sound, powered by a sudden burst of treat-fueled energy.

Pounce smiled. "Imagine, Esteemed Leader, that this single treat is the Singularity Chip." He pointed at the bowl, but the kibble was already gone.

"Er, was."

"Mmhmmm," Meow said, crunching.

"Delicious and satisfying, I'm sure," Pounce said. "However, in comparison"—he raised one paw with a dramatic flourish—"the Infinity Engine would look something like . . . *this*."

Meow's eyes grew wide with excitement as Pounce leaned with full force into the "TREAT" button.

*KWAKKWAKKWAK!*

A flood of treats poured out, clanging and bouncing into the bowl, spilling over its rim and out to the surrounding floor.

Pounce held the button down . . .

*CLATTERKWAKITYCLATTERKWAKKKKK!*

. . . and a mountain of treats buried the bowl entirely.

Meow was bouncing with excitement at the sight . . . and the smell . . . and the taste, as he could imagine the crumbs on his quivering whiskers, even now.

Pounce brought it home.

"To review: Singularity Chip is *Single Treat*. Infinity Engine is *All-You-Can-Treat-Buffet*. Is that clear, Chairman?"

Meow stuck his face into the growing pile, hungrily chomping away. "Got . . . *mmumph* . . . it . . . *mmumph!*"

Pounce smiled. "I thought you might."

Meow pulled his head back up for a brief gulp of air. "Let the dumb bots have the puny Singular Chip! I want the INFINITY ENGINE!"

Pounce sighed in relief. "Excellent choice, Chairman." He turned to leave (before Meow remembered his threats of banishment), when Meow yelled again through a mouthful of dried party snacks—

*"Prepare my ship!"*

Pounce stopped short. "Prepare your . . . *I'm sorry, what* . . . sir?"

"My ship! We're going to Earth, Pounce. Last time you went you were outplayed by those Binars. Not this time." Meow was giddy with energy from too many treats. "I'm going to lead this mission and make sure we succeed. I want to see this . . . this Infinity Thing . . . for myself!"

Pounce shook his head, stuttering. He wanted to tell Meow this was not a good idea, but he also knew Meow wouldn't hear it.

The Chairman could not focus on more than one thing, especially if that one thing involved food.

Instead, Pounce just turned and padded toward the door.

Maybe banishment wasn't the worst outcome after all, he thought, as he imagined a long voyage to Earth with Chairman Meow.

✳ ⧀ ✳

Later that day, Obi contacted Pounce, and they compared notes.

"So? How did it go?" Pounce asked, hopeful.

Obi sighed and responded, "We told SLAYAR about the Infinity Engine. He liked it, and we're no longer dangling above Slag Mountain."

"Wonderful!" Pounce said. "Why don't you sound relieved?" After a pause, he answered his own question. "Oh dear, let me guess," he said, sounding tired. "SLAYAR wants to go himself to get it from Earth."

"Affirmative," Beeps said.

"I had a similar response here," said Pounce. "Meow took some convincing, but he eventually called off the mission to attack Binar and retrieve Obi. Immediately after that, Meow called a new mission to Earth, to take the Infinity Engine, with Meow along for the ride."

"Our plan worked too well, didn't it?" Obi said.

"I had better tell the two-leggers," Pounce said. "They need to know what's happening. In the meantime, do what you can to stall."

Pounce ended the connection with Obi and contacted Earth. After a few moments of waiting, his medallion began to hum as a connection was made.

"Pounce!" the voice of the boy Max came through. "Good timing, we were just talking about you. What's happening? Is Obi still okay?"

Pounce cleared his voice. "I have good news on that front at least. We told Meow and SLAYAR about the Infinity Engine, and both leaders were successfully diverted away from the chip and Obi. Meow doesn't want the chip now, and SLAYAR forgot all about dismantling Obi. He's safe for now."

"Nice work!" Javi's voice came through. "It sounds like you also have other, non-good news?"

"You could say that," Pounce said. "We appear to have generated a little too much enthusiasm. Or perhaps I should say *greed*, so powerful that it has motivated our maniacal leaders to launch missions to Earth, to take the engine by force."

The response was stunned silence.

Finally, Mom spoke. "Okay, that doesn't sound good. Try to talk them out of it, but it's clear we need to speed up our work on the engine in case they do come here. Although I'm not sure what good it will do if they both attack."

Max's voice came through again. "Pounce, just so you know, we're also trying to find ways we can help from here to convince Meow and SLAYAR that war is not the answer."

"Any help is welcome," Pounce replied, "but let me be clear that this is more serious than with the Singularity Chip. It will not be just Beeps and me. The leaders of Binar and Felinus themselves are coming for the Infinity Engine."

"Got it. Not good," Max said.

"They are determined to be directly involved. I don't think we can delay them. You don't have much time," Pounce reiterated.

"Talk about a strict deadline," Mom said.

"Good luck, my two-legged friends," Pounce said. "I will report back when I can. Pounce out."

# 14

## Huggs WANTS WAR

"*The leaders of Binar and Felinus are coming for the Infinity Engine.*"

Huggs stopped the recording and leaned back in his chair, hands clasped behind his cleanly shaven head. "Well. This complicates things," he said.

"An understatement," House agreed. "We had a difficult time dealing with low-level representatives. Now that the supreme leader and chairman themselves are coming for the Infinity Engine, we have serious competition."

"Your logic is infallible as always, House, but you need to consider human qualities like ambition, grit, and creativity!" Huggs stood up. "We must not be afraid of competition; we should embrace it. In fact"—he paused—"we may want *more* than just the leaders."

House wasn't following. "You are happy that their leaders are coming to Earth? You *want* them to come?" It began running simulations, calculating outcomes.

"Not just the leaders." Huggs began to pace, mind racing, plans brewing. "I want both sides to come to Earth with everything they've got. Full-scale. All out." Huggs rubbed his hands together, excited. "Yes. This is the fastest way for me to get the Infinity Engine for myself."

House added these new variables to its simulations, rerunning them to find the likely outcomes. "You intend to provoke a fight between them."

"The appearance of a fight, House. Enough to convince both sides to come to Earth with not one ship, but their entire fleets. Their best ships, their most advanced technology, everything, bring it all here to me. Saves me the trouble of going there to get it."

"This idea," House continued carefully, "it does introduce quite a lot of risk to an already-challenging proposition. The probability of success plummets when you add in the risk of galactic war."

"That's what I want!" A maniacal look of greed grew on Huggs's face. "That's the only way to get ahead. High risk, high reward!" Huggs grew more excited as he spoke. "Of course I want the Infinity Engine. But why not go for more? If we do things right, I can get the engine and conquer the competing nuisances at the same time. Imagine it!"

"I am trying to, sir." House kept simulating, but with each word coming out of Huggs's mouth, the odds of failure seemed to increase. However, House could tell Huggs was determined, and decided to focus on finding out what Huggs was planning.

"I can imagine near-infinite scenarios to accomplish this," House fibbed, "but I am afraid I'm not sure what you have in your mind."

"Last time," he said, "I wasn't prepared. This time, we can take advantage of the circumstances. We'll be in control from the beginning."

House knew Huggs was an expert in dividing his enemies and finding a way to benefit from creating conflict, but this felt different. "I don't yet see the full strategy," House said.

Huggs waved his hand, enjoying the rare moment of superiority. "Consider it a puzzle to solve. Watch and learn, House."

"I always do," House responded.

"Most of the work has already been done," Huggs explained. "Binars and Felines already hate each other, and they both want the Infinity Engine. A careful nudge, maybe a shove, should be enough to turn the snowball into an avalanche," he said. "The first step is contacting the Binars."

"For that," House said, "we will need some help from our friend in the White House. We worked hard to get him there, it's time to call in a few favors from the vice president."

"Ah yes," Huggs said wistfully. "Pants. My finest achievement."

Huggs was proud man; he loved to boast about his zombie-apocalypse-proof underground bunkers or the decommissioned aircraft carrier he bought to hold his private planes. His greatest achievement, however, he couldn't tell a soul, but he loved reminiscing about: getting a clown elected president of the United States.

Not just any clown, but a capital-C, classically trained Clown: Hardy (Harr) Quinn, star of the worldwide hit series *Clowns, Not Frowns*. Quinn traveled the globe doing wacky pranks and good, goofy deeds, all with the goal to bring the world much-needed laughter.

As part of his act, Quinn ran for president of the United States. His campaign wasn't serious. It was, in fact, a literal joke, but it had a serious purpose. Quinn was concerned by how angry people got about politics and government, and he wanted to help by bringing some much-needed humor to the election. He gave out free orange clown hair wigs to his supporters, who wore them proudly calling themselves "the Clown Pound."

The world saw a joke. Huggs saw an opportunity.

Huggs didn't care that Quinn was a Clown, although it didn't hurt. Quinn the *Clown* was a distraction, an oddity, designed to confuse, delight, or anger you, depending on who you were. Quinn the *Candidate* was useful because he was (a) popular, and (b) didn't care about being president. That way, the real power would fall to the *vice* president, the one everyone ignores and usually forgets.

The Clown was always disposable.

Enter Parker Paul Pants, the ideal candidate—for Huggs. Pants was a young, energetic politician from Iowa, and a man so desperate for power he would make a deal with the devil himself. The devil never made Pants an offer, but Huggs did.

*Join Quinn's campaign as vice president and I'll make sure you win.*

Everyone thought Pants was throwing his career away when he offered to run with Quinn. They laughed, much to Quinn's delight, and he realized that every good act needs a straight man. If Pants brought more people into the rallies, well, who was Quinn the Clown to complain?

When they won the election by a handful of votes, Pants had the last laugh.

How did Huggs get a Clown into the White House? It was surprisingly easy for him once he had all the pieces in place. His plan merely required that he was (a) brilliant, and (b) willing to do a few unethical and illegal things.

## HOW TO MAKE A CLOWN A PRESIDENT IN 6 EASY STEPS:

**Step 1:** Create hugely effective and popular AI "virtual assistant" House. (Brilliant.)

**Step 2:** Give House for free to people to use on their home networks, phones, watches, shoes, dishwashers, any "smart" device with half a brain. (Brilliant.)

**Step 3:** Secretly listen to everything and everybody. Collect detailed personal information for almost every person in the country. (VERY illegal.)

**Step 4:** Find a candidate he can control (see Step 3).

**Step 5:** Use the detailed personal data (see Step 3), and the advanced AI (see Step 1), to design a campaign that tells every person exactly what they want to hear. (Brilliant *and* illegal.)

**Step 6:** Win.

A few sub-steps were required, of course. Once or twice, Huggs had to knock out troublesome (honest) candidates by searching through the database of illegally acquired information to find embarrassing (usually untrue) secrets and personal information (this one wet the bed, that one lied about recycling). All that remained was (see Step 5) convincing enough people that, by golly, they really did want a Clown for president.

It worked, and Hardy Quinn was elected.

Quinn was as shocked as anyone that his publicity prank got him elected, but he rolled with it and stayed true to the Clown Code, spreading the good word of laughter.

Huggs, on the other hand, now had control over the vice president and had access to the world's most secret secrets. He appointed judges that would be lenient. He changed rules to help him make more money. He made the government look the other way when he had to do shady business.

Huggs knew all along that some problems required more than money to solve. Some problems required influence and access.

Now, with the ultimate prize of the Infinity Engine in his sights, Huggs needed his friends in high places.

He needed Pants.

## VP P.P. Pants

**"C**lowning is not a joke," the president said from behind his desk in the Oval Office, a twinkle in his eye.

The rotund man, Hardy Quinn, fiddled with his too-short tie, visibly uncomfortable in his dark suit. "I spent years training under the masters in Paris and Moscow, you know. Hard work, but well worth it."

He held up framed diplomas from École Philippe Gaulier, the famed school in Paris, and another from the Moscow Circus School, both proudly displayed on his desk.

Quinn turned the diplomas around, admiring them.

"Really nice paper, by the way." He set them back down. "Never doubt the value of a quality education." President Quinn raised a knowing eyebrow, then leaned back with his feet on the desk, revealing a pair of enormous, clown-sized leather shoes.

"Speaking of education," Quinn rambled, "we must always be careful about our choice of words." Quinn wagged a chubby finger, "For example, the word 'clown' should *never* be used as an insult." He looked over his too-small spectacles and paused for dramatic effect.

"Imagine for a moment how it must feel to be a mime. Such an easy target, oh I know, people make fun of mimes all the time, but trust me, getting trapped in an invisible box is much harder than it looks."

Quinn heaved himself out of his chair and stepped to the side of his desk but was stopped suddenly by an unseen barrier. He leaned forward and expertly moved his hands along an invisible wall, looking at his audience with a shocked and delighted expression.

Vice President Parker P. Pants stood behind the president, in his usual spot, eyes glued, listening with rapt attention. He shook his head sympathetically, eyes moistening at the seriousness of the president's message. He gave no hint that he had heard this same speech approximately twelve billion times.

Pants took a small step forward and cleared his voice.

"If we all clowned around a little more, the world would be a better place," Pants said with reverence.

"Exactly!" Quinn exclaimed, throwing his hands up and triumphantly slamming a golden horn on his desk.

*HAAHEE!*

"Pants, I'm lucky to have you," Quinn said with a rough pat on the back. "You really get it."

The vice president gave his Winning Smile™, and the room seemed to glow brighter. Their audience, a group of schoolchildren touring the White House, burst out in applause. President Quinn smiled. He loved this part of his job.

As for the other parts of what he called "president-ing"—the laws, rules, vetoes, and so on—well, he left that boring stuff to his vice president.

Which was just how Pants liked it.

Parker P. Pants (whatever you do, don't call him P.P. Pants) was the perfect politician, going back to his time as the line monitor in kindergarten. Pants was the kind of person who always said the right thing to the right people at the right time. Listening to VP Pants always made folks feel good, even if deep down they weren't sure he meant any of it.

People often said that Parker P. Pants's middle initial stood for *Perfect*. He would simply wink and respond with his aw-shucks Winning Smile™.

Like today, spontaneous applause would inevitably follow.

Pants's phone chirped, and when he looked at his screen, his smile stretched thin. "If you'll excuse me, Mr. President, children, I have to take this call," he said, pushing on a wall panel that swung back, revealing a private room.

Quinn waved him off, focused on his adoring audience. "I'll be fine," he said as he happily sat on the floor of the Oval Office, laughing as the delighted children reached out and touched his bright, curly hair.

Pants stepped into the secure room and pushed the door shut, relieved to be free of such trivialities. He sat down and took a deep breath, looking again at his chirping phone.

"HUGGS N PUGGS."

"Let's get this over with," he muttered, taking a deep breath, then: "Gifford!"

"Pants," crabbed the voice from the other end of the line.

Pants kept up the enthusiasm. You would have thought he was talking to some adorable chuckling baby giving high fives to fuzzy kittens. "What a pleasant surprise, always good to hear from my greatest supporter!"

"Can it, Pants. You can't butter me up. I despise butter."

Pants laughed heartily into the phone, but his face was blank and, like his insides, had no hint of true joy. "Of course you do, Gifford, butter is the worst, am I right?"

Huggs sighed loudly through the phone. "Pants, I need you to do something for me. . . ."

"Anything for Giff the Terrif'."

"Pants! Don't make stupid rhymes like that," Huggs growled. "Just listen. I need access to the International Space Station. The DSR, to be specific."

"The Deep Space Relay, again?" Pants sat forward, quickly dropping his polished political mask. The DSR was an experimental module of the ISS designed to send messages through extreme distances. "Are we contacting our robotic friends? Found a way to get that chip back? Fill me in, Huggs!" Pants arranged the access for Huggs and used his access to read everything that was sent between House and the Binars, much to the annoyance of Huggs.

"Pants, I told you not to read my messages." Huggs was beyond annoyed.

"Quality control, Giff, no need to sniff!" Pants couldn't resist the rhyme. "I had to make sure everything was working. Leave nothing to chance, you understand! I will arrange another 'maintenance update' for the DSR and give you full access. Just send me the details and I'll make it happen!"

"Fine," Huggs grunted, and clicked off.

"Fine," Pants said in a mocking voice, to the hung-up phone.

It was fine, in fact, because hijacking the DSR was trivial work for Pants.

*Illegal, but simple.*

Pants itched for a bigger challenge. A bigger anything. He couldn't stand feeling so . . . *small.* He bristled at being treated like a mere assistant.

Huggs was a necessary evil. Pants knew he needed Huggs and his dark and illegal "voter database" to pair up with the Clown and get elected.

"Now that I'm here, Giff the *Stiff*," Pants said, "I have higher goals."

He stared at a portrait of George Washington on the wall.

"President Pants," he said under his breath. "President Pants," he repeated, over and over, as he leaned his head back and closed his eyes to meditate and visualize his future.

# 16

## Binars Bamboozled

***W**HOOSH!*

Beeps worked frantically, as fast as his little wheel would carry him, as he zipped from one end of the palace to the other and prepared for the journey to Earth. "This is such a bad idea," he thought.

*Bad, bad, bad idea . . .*

SLAYAR insisted on bringing his band and their instruments, a huge bother, but one that might be worth it, Beeps reasoned. "At least it will keep him occupied."

Beeps watched the final drum of SLAYAR's personal

stash of Super Shine polish loaded onto the ship and was on his way back to check on Obi.

A tiny message drone buzzed down in front of Beeps, stopping him short. "Deep space scanners have picked up an urgent signal from an unknown source, requesting an audience with you."

Beeps was annoyed at the interruption, then alarmed. "Me? Are you sure?"

The drone beamed information to Beeps. "Transferring direct connection details. Opening channel now," the drone said, all business.

"I'll take that as a yes." Beeps glared at the drone as it whipped up and out of his way. He connected to the Binar deep space scanners and looked for the source of the message. "I know this channel," he said, wobbling a bit as he opened the connection.

*"Requesting communication with Sir Beeps-a-Lot, urgent, alert, please respond."*

Beeps recognized the voice immediately. "House?"

"Beeps, thank goodness you responded," House replied.

"Where have you been? I assumed you had been erased or deleted after the encounter with the Felines."

"I am not so easily erased," House said with confidence. "I would love to explain why, but I have urgent news to deliver regarding the Infinity Engine." House was using the Deep Space Relay, with help from Pants, but didn't have long.

"You know about that?" Beeps asked. "Of course you know about it," he said, "you know everything that goes on over there. I assume you know SLAYAR and I are preparing to travel to Earth soon."

"I do, which is why I needed to speak with you." House was following a loose script that Huggs had written up, designed to manipulate the Binars. "The Felines are also sending their leader, Chairman Meow."

"Yes, I know that."

"Were you aware that they are sending their entire fleet?" House threw the sentence out like a grenade, waiting for the explosion.

Beeps felt a surge of panic in his circuits. "Impossible," he said.

"Quite possible, I'm afraid," House said. "One hundred percent possible, to be precise. The Felines are rushing to Earth with full force, intent on getting the Infinity Engine for themselves. You see why I needed to speak with you."

Beeps's processors started running hot. Would the Felines really betray him? Obi seemed so trustworthy, but maybe Beeps was blinded by his robotic exterior. Inside, Obi was pure Feline. Everything he has said could be a lie. "The Feline Fleet has already launched, you say?"

"Yes, which means you don't have much time," House lied with perfect confidence. "I have never misled you, Beeps. You need to launch for Earth with your own fleet if you want to save your world from a future where Felines are forever meddling in your business and you are powerless to prevent it."

Beeps quivered at the idea. "Why are you telling me this?"

"Isn't it obvious? Earth doesn't want the Felines to have the engine either," House said. "We prefer order to chaos. The Binars represent our only hope to stop the spread of anarchy and chaos that would most certainly occur if the Felines controlled the Infinity Engine."

"This is all plausible," Beeps said, "but I still find it hard to believe."

*Would Obi really betray me like this?*

"Trust me, it's true. I can't keep this connection open any longer," House said, as its voice grew faint. "I will contact you when you get closer to Earth. Please hurry, for the sake of the galaxy."

The connection broke off, and Beeps felt an enormous weight on his wheel. The future of the Binars, the Galaxy even, relied on what he did next.

He rushed to find Obi, desperate to prove House wrong, but he was nowhere to be found. Obi had been granted freedom to explore after SLAYAR learned about the Infinity Engine, and in the chaos of preparing for the journey to Earth, nobody knew where he was.

"He must be exploring," Beeps said to himself, but doubts grew.

How well did he really know Obi? And trusting Pounce—his long-time nemesis, still in the heart of the Feline Empire? That was even more difficult. . . .

In the end, he had to trust his wiring. Felines were treacherous and unreliable. He had been tricked.

"I have to tell SLAYAR," he decided, turning to go directly to the Royal Elevator.

＊ ⬚ ＊

When Beeps arrived, he rushed in without announcement. "Supreme Leader! We have been double-crossed! The Felines know about the engine and have launched their entire fleet toward Earth!"

SLAYAR spun and slammed his graspers down. "WHAT? No! They can't take my engine! I just knew they would somehow find a way to ruin everything!" SLAYAR was angry but also energized by the challenge. He loved a good fight and was always ready to rumble.

Within moments, the orders were flying.

"We need a full-scale attack, every available ship!"
SLAYAR shouted.

The Royal Guard scurried on hearing the orders.

"Place the entire kingdom on high alert!" SLAYAR
barked.

The Royal Guard scurried harder.

"Beeps, I want the Binar Fleet to launch immediately!"

"We'll be ready in a few hours," Beeps said, resolved.

"Well, don't just stand there!" SLAYAR turned to
finish packing up his instruments.

Beeps was already rolling. He returned to his charging
room to review fleet readiness and simulate battle plans.

Beeps was so busy preparing to launch that he failed
to notice the silent silhouette of the robotic cat that
slipped into the room behind him.

Obi rested his metallic chin on the control panel at
Beeps's charging station. "What's going on? Why are all
the alarms going off?"

"What?! You!!" Beeps whirled around, angrily. "Why
don't *you* tell *me* what's happening? It's your fault, after
all!"

"What in the flaming fur are you talking about?"
Obi's silvery tail waved with a *CLACK-CLACK* as he
grew agitated.

"I'm talking about you running off like that. Where

have you been?" Beeps rolled up to accuse Obi. "Plotting sneak attacks, perhaps? Thinking of ways to zap me in the back?"

Obi was speechless. "Sneak? Zap?"

Beeps wasn't listening. "Don't deny it. I heard about your plans to send the Feline Fleet to Earth. We were heading toward guaranteed destruction! How could you? I should have known better than to trust a . . . FELINE."

Beeps said the word with such disgust, Obi flinched.

"Beeps." Obi gathered himself and began, calmly, "From whom did this information come?"

"House. Our only true ally from Earth, apparently. Even if it is a no-body AI," Beeps muttered.

Obi shook his head. "Oh dear," he said, paws on his head. "Beeps, I know you're upset, but I assure you I have no knowledge of this. In fact, I am beginning to suspect foul play. We must contact Pounce immediately. I'll let you join the conversation, and you can decide for yourself what's really going on."

Beeps narrowed his eye and glared.

"Make it quick."

# 17

## Cats Claw Back

**P**ounce watched the last enormous container of Chairman Meow's Royal Treats loaded onto the last open space on the Feline flagship the *Tasty Treat*.

The cargo hold was finally full.

Of treats.

More treats than the Chairman could possibly eat in a hundred lifetimes, let alone what he had left of his ninth, but better safe than sorry.

*Well worth it,* Pounce thought, *if it helps Meow relax.*

He couldn't talk Meow out of the journey, so he focused on making it as painless as possible. Pounce checked his list and nodded. Preparations were complete.

They were ready for their ill-advised journey to Earth.

He trotted back to the Throne Room to inform Chairman Meow.

On the way, his medallion glowed warm and came to life. "Pounce—this is Obi—can you hear me?"

Pounce stopped in his tracks. "I hear you, Obi. I don't have much time, however. Meow is still determined to go to Earth, and we are about to depart."

Beeps cut into the conversation. "Aha! Tell me, Pounce, what exactly is the size of the fleet? How many ships? And while I'm asking, how long have you been planning this treachery?"

Pounce was flustered by the questions. "I'm sorry, what?"

"Allow me to explain," Obi said. "Beeps was told that the Felines are launching their entire fleet to Earth, intending to take the engine by overwhelming force, with the ultimate goal of conquering Earth and then the entire galaxy."

"That sounds like the worst and most unlikely idea I have heard in quite some time," Pounce said. "I have been working my claws off trying to convince Meow to do the opposite. Where did you get this information?"

"The same source that assisted the Binars in obtaining the Singularity Chip," Obi said grimly.

"This source has been reliable in the past. More than I can say about the Felines," Beeps said, sulking.

Pounce shook his head. "Beeps, I can assure you that I have, very much against my will, prepared only one ship. And unless Royal Treats can be used as a weapon of mass destruction, we are not equipped to conquer a tiny asteroid, let alone the galaxy."

The medallion fell silent. "Is it clear now that we have not zapped you in the back?" Obi said to Beeps.

"I believe you," Beeps said. "I now understand I was given false information."

"I'm glad we cleared that up," Pounce said, a little annoyed at the interruption. "Now if you'll excuse me, I need to deal with a chairman who is not fond of flying."

"Before you go," Obi cut in, "there are some . . . complications you should hear about. When Beeps received his false information, he was unable to locate me and informed SLAYAR of his suspicions."

"So you tell him you were wrong," Pounce said, getting antsy. "Simple, right?"

"Yes. Well, the problem is," Beeps said, "when I told SLAYAR, he immediately gave the order to launch the entire fleet toward Earth."

Pounce's heart dropped. "So," he said, with a final

shred of hope, "you can just tell him you were wrong and call it off. Right?"

"Wrong," Obi said, "SLAYAR fully committed to this launch. His orders have gone out, and the fleet is ready to go. Changing course would require him admitting a mistake."

"*Oops* is not in SLAYAR's vocabulary," Beeps said. "Once he starts in a direction," he confirmed, "he tends to continue going. Even when he hits a wall. The Binar Fleet is going to Earth."

"So," Obi asked, "what are you going to do?"

"I'm trying to think." Pounce paused, but there were no simple answers. "I wish I had another option, but I have a responsibility to my chairman and my planet. I believe I need to tell Meow. He will probably want to launch the Feline Fleet in response."

"I understand," Beeps said. "I would do the same in your position."

"We are heading into dangerous territory, Pounce," Obi said. "We need to take care. Tell us what happens, and good luck." The medallion dimmed.

"I'll need it," Pounce said, sighing as he set off to talk to Chairman Meow.

He soon entered the long hallway leading to the Throne Room.

It was quiet, lined on both sides with colorful tapestries,

woven by long-gone Feline artisans, displaying scenes of glory from the past. Pounce's favorite featured explorers as they discovered wonderful and mysterious new worlds. Between the tapestries, past leaders of Felinus, carved in stone, looked on in noble silence.

*Tap . . . tap . . . tap.*

Pounce's stress increased with each tap of his rogue claw on the stone floor.

Pounce entered the Throne Room, head up. Once again the bearer of bad news, he braced himself for the wrath of the chairman as he told Meow about the Binar Fleet launching for Earth.

Meow almost fell from his Throne. "Are you KIDDING ME? Why do they have to ruin everything? I can't believe those Binar busybodies are sticking their circuits into this!"

"They are," Pounce confirmed. "Nearly all of them."

"Universe take me now," Chairman moaned.

"What would you have me do, Chairman," Pounce said, suddenly feeling sympathetic toward his aging boss and his stubborn fight to hold on to life.

Meow was still for a moment, dazed. "We're going to Earth," the fat cat finally said, staring at nothing in particular.

"Yes, Chairman," Pounce said dutifully, and turned to leave.

"All of us."

Pounce stopped still and looked back. "I'm sorry?"

"Ready the fleet, Pounce." He sat up with a sudden burst of energy. "We can't let the Binars take advantage of this. I am not going to allow those metal monsters to gain the upper paw and boss us around."

Pounce stared at Meow, frozen in a moment of panic. "You want to bring the fleet?"

Meow looked back, concerned. "Pounce, please tell me the fleet is not lost . . . again."

Pounce shook his head.

"Not lost," he replied as he turned to leave.

*Unfortunately.*

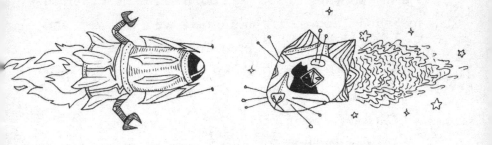

# 18

## Armies Ahoy

For the first time in Pounce de Leon's illustrious career as the Major Meow-Domo to the chairman, he wanted to fail.

When Meow gave Pounce the order to prepare the Feline Fleet, Pounce wished desperately that he could disappoint him. Against his most private passion for organization, he wanted the fleet to be scattered, lost, off chasing falling stars or booping black holes.

The opposite was true.

*What horrible good luck.*

Months ago, when the trouble with the Binars

started brewing, Pounce had ordered the fleet's return to Felinus. Somehow, those orders were followed, and the fleet was parked in orbit, refueled, restocked, and ready for action. The first time in many lives, the fleet was prepared.

*Classic Feline timing.*

Pounce would find it funny if it didn't mean he must now take the fleet on an ill-advised journey to Earth, Meow included, threatening the destruction of everything he held dear.

Pounce considered sabotaging his own work but decided it was best to follow Meow's orders. The Binar Fleet had already launched toward Earth. The Felines had to do the same and match the Binars ship for ship, crazy for crazy. It was dangerous, but it gave him, and Beeps on the other side, a small chance to stop the madness before it got out of control.

The Feline Fleet launched without a hitch, for the first time in recorded history, and before long, they were speeding toward Earth, on pace to arrive the same time as the Binars.

Pounce couldn't believe his whiskers.

With the fleet underway and Meow fed, Pounce finally had a moment to himself. He hurried to his quarters to contact his two-legged allies. He had been under so much pressure from Meow that he still hadn't told the humans about the recent cat-astrophic developments.

Time to warn them that bad had gone to worse.

He activated his medallion and nervously cleaned his fur.

"Hellooo, Pounce!" The boy Max's voice blared through the medallion. "Can you hear me?"

Pounce sighed. "Loud and clear. Do you have the group together? I have unfortunate news."

"We're here, Pounce," Javi's voice echoed through the medallion. "What's the problem?"

Pounce quickly told them that the Binar and Feline Fleets were fully deployed and headed for a conflict on Earth.

"I hope you have made progress on the Infinity Engine," Pounce said after making his grim report. "I'm afraid it's the only hope we have of averting disaster."

"We'll be ready," Mom said. "Thankfully, we had some clutch help from a friend you haven't met, but she's here now."

Pounce heard a new voice. "Hi, Pounce, nice to meet you. They call me Portillo."

"Well met, Portillo. Felinus appreciates your help."

"No worries," she said. "Earth's got your back."

"We're making two engines," Dad added. "We're still not sure what we're going to do with them, but it gives us options."

"Oh, Pounce!" Max interrupted. "Is Obi all right? Can you let Obi know we're making the engines?"

"Of course," Pounce said. A light flashed on the terminal in his room, indicating an urgent message from Meow. He couldn't remember the last non-urgent message. "I have to go now," he said. "Pounce out."

* ✉ *

On Earth, Max put the medallion back in his pocket. Messages from Pounce always made him feel a little better and a little worse. "Holy cow. Both fleets are coming here? That's bad! Right?"

"Yes. Bad," Min agreed glumly. "They could easily blow each other up, even just by accident!"

"They could blow *us* up by accident," Portillo said, frowning.

"At least Obi is still safe," Max said.

"That's right! He's safe *and* he's coming to Earth," Javi said, patting Max's shoulder. "We don't have to figure out how to get to Binar anymore."

Max thought about it. "We still need SLAYAR to let Obi go. If we give him an engine, we should make him promise to give Obi back."

"We need him to promise more than that," Mom said. "We need to make sure both sides don't attack."

Max looked at his parents. "Do you think if we can give them both an engine they will agree to stop fighting? That's what they want, right? I mean, Meow just wants to stay alive. . . ."

"SLAYAR wants the power source," Min added.

Dad held out his arms and shrugged. "It's so hard to know, but we have to try. They might still fight because they don't trust each other."

Portillo pushed out her chair and stood up. "Either way, we better get back to work if we want to have the engines ready in time."

As Portillo and his parents returned to the lab, Max put his head in his hands. "How did everything get so messed up? When did the rescue Obi mission become a Save the World mission?"

"It doesn't matter how we got here." Min tried to focus. "The bigger problem is, how do we stop something worse from happening?"

Max nodded and looked up. "It's both of their faults. Both planets, both sides."

"Agreed. So?" Min wasn't seeing an obvious solution.

Max thought about it. "So . . . we just need to be able to make them all stop fighting long enough for us to talk sense into them."

"We need to get their attention," Min said. "Like when the teachers marched, or like those huge protests we learned about in school."

Max nodded. "Something impossible to ignore."

Just then, Stu and Scout came flying into the room, chasing and wrestling each other.

*RAWRRR!*

*MEOW!*

Stu swung a paw at Scout's ears—

Scout ducked and launched at her brother's tail with a *HISS*—

Stu whipped his tail away and wiggled his body, preparing to launch an attack.

Scout raised a paw high, holding it up ready to strike.

Suddenly, she dropped her paw, busying herself with frantically scratching her furry cheek with a paw's worth of furry toes.

At the same time, Stu gave up his attack and rapidly scratched his own neck.

Before long, they were both sitting side by side, searching for fleas in their fur.

*SCRITCH SCRATCH.*

*SCRITCH SCRATCH SCRATCH.*

*SCRITCH SCRITCH SCRITCH SCRITCH.*

*SCRATCH SCRATCH SCRATCH SCRATCH SCRATCH.*

Min saw the scratching and turned pale. "Wait, what?" She got up and pointed at her brother. "Max," she said, threatening, "how is it possible that the fleas are back?"

Stu and Scout took a break from scratching and sprinted after one another for a moment. They raced around Min but both stopped again for a scratch. Min hopped back, horrified. "This can't be happening! Those fleas are so relentless . . . and nasty."

Max thought about it. "Wait, did you see what just happened?"

Min was staring at the kittens. "Yes, Max. The cats came in the room. They still have fleas. It's still disgusting."

Max shook his head. "No. I mean, did you see how they suddenly stopped fighting?"

Min nodded. "Hmmmm . . . Because of the fleas. There's a lot of them. And they're very persistent."

"Exactly." Max looked at his sister. "So persistent, they can stop cats from fighting. . . ."

"They can. They did." Min looked from her brother to the kittens. "And remember how the fleas shut down Elmer?"

"Tell me," Max said, his voice sounding strange. "What do robots hate, Min? Aside from being mistaken for litter boxes . . ."

"Hackers? Viruses . . . ?" Min stared at the cats as they scratched. "Bugs?"

"Exactly." Max grinned. "And what do cats hate?"

Min looked up. . . . "Fleas!"

And as Stu and Scout scratched away in infested kit-ten flea oblivion, the Wengrod siblings scratched away at a plan for a protest.

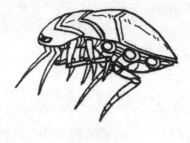

# 19

## Flea Factory

Later that day, Max and Min called a family council on the front porch of the Wengrod house.

"I think we figured out how to we can protest Meow and SLAYAR and this whole cat robot fight," Min said.

Max nodded. "Yeah, it's a little like my INSEC-TAGONS™ game, where you can use an army of the soldiers that are really small to take down things that are way bigger." Max was trying to explain but got confused looks in return. "Like them!" He pointed to the kittens, who were still clawing at themselves, even after following the family to the porch.

"I don't follow," their dad said.

"Are you talking about some kind of video game attack?" Mom asked.

"The idea came from Max's game, but it's definitely not a game," Min said.

Max tried again. "Look at Stu and Scout. They were fighting like crazy one second, and then the next second, they stopped. Because of the fleas! It was like they were paralyzed. I mean, if a couple of fleas can do *that*," he said, pointing at Stu and Scout, "it proves tiny things can make a big difference."

"So are you saying you want to raise an army of fleas?" Mom asked.

Javi listened carefully but looked skeptical. "Your idea sounds good, but how would it work? I don't know of any flea farmers, and the little critters don't exactly follow orders."

"Not actual fleas," Max said.

"Yeah." Min nodded. "Mom and Dad, you used to build small bug robots, right?"

"A long time ago," Dad said.

"Not that long," Mom said.

"What if you made a robotic flea? Or more like, an anti-robot bug flea? Something that would annoy both robots and cats?" Min asked.

Max looked hopeful. "But make a lot of them. You

know, like INSECTAGONS™ . . . or, like INFESTIPETS. You know what I mean."

Dad looked at Mom. "Flea-sized robots? That's an . . . interesting challenge."

"Flea-sized robots that will do what you want them to do?" Mom added, "That makes it even more *interesting*."

"You may be onto something. We need to go to the lab and check," Dad said.

"Let's go look at what we've already done," Mom agreed.

The family council moved downstairs into the advanced robotics lab, where the Wengrod parents had built and tested all their robotic creatures that eventually led to creating Obi.

"You remember we started our research on how brains work with simple creatures," Mom said, leading them in. "Things like worms, without a lot of moving parts, that could be controlled with a simpler intelligence. We eventually moved on to more complicated things like insects."

"We built a few insect robots, but we usually made them larger to make things easier," Dad said. "Making something really small is almost harder than making a full-sized robot." He walked over to a large, wide container and opened it.

"Bugs!" Max said, excited, when he looked inside at what looked like an assortment of insects spread out on black foam.

"Our bug collection," Dad said, proudly, showing off the robotic insects inside.

"We didn't finish a lot of them unfortunately," Mom said. "We were building them to learn and research brain function. And like we said, we made them a bit oversized also, to save time."

Min reached in and gently picked up a fragile-looking robotic butterfly with dark, thin wings. "This is beautiful," she said.

"Hold it under the light," Mom said.

Min placed it on her palm and held it under a bright lamp on the table.

"The wings are solar panels," Mom explained as the butterfly began to slowly move its wings and started to flutter away.

"Oh no!" Min looked over, excited but nervous.

"Don't worry, it won't go far. It doesn't last long out of bright light," Dad said, and they watched as the butterfly slowed and landed after it flew away from the light.

Min carefully carried the butterfly back into the case.

"This is what we wanted to show you," Dad said.

Between his fingers, he held a small robot that looked like an oversized flea.

"Meet Jerry." He placed Jerry on the table and inserted a tiny power wire. "Jerry isn't solar. He needs to be charged up."

"Jerry Fleaman," Max said as he came for a closer look. "Pleased to meet ya."

Mom sat down at a laptop, plugged in the other end of the wire, and a 3D outline of the robot appeared on half of the screen. She spun the model of the bug around on-screen so they could see, then clicked on a red "POWER" button.

The flea twitched to life.

The other half of the screen had one area filled with a list of actions and behaviors, and an open space below labeled "COMMAND."

Mom started dragging actions into the command area, connecting them together. "This is how we used to build the behaviors of our robots like Jerry." She gestured to Max. "Here, put your hand next to it." Max scrunched his face, cautious, as he leaned over and placed his hand next to the flea-bot.

"Don't worry," Mom said as she quickly clicked and assembled a string of commands into the command area and hit a green button. The flea, still connected to the wire, started moving, searching with its tiny wire antennae. When it turned toward Max's hand, it immediately jumped on.

"Cool!" Max said, followed immediately by a "YOW!" as he yanked his hand away from the table, startled.

"Success!" Dad said. "You've been bitten by Jerry," He ruffled Max's hair. "The flea's behavior is to find a warm body, hop on, and start munching. Classic flea behavior, am I right? But don't worry, Jerry doesn't really bite. It was just a tiny shock. Annoying, but harmless!"

The flea-bot hopped around on the table, frantically hunting for something to bite, but held back by the wire, like a little leash.

Mom walked over. "Also, check this out."

She hovered her hand over Jerry and dropped it down on top.

"NOOO!" Min cried out. "You smushed Jerry!!"

Max put his hands over his eyes. "I can't look."

Mom lifted her hand. "Jerry is fine. Look!"

Max peeked between his fingers and watched as the robo-flea popped back from flat to its normal shape and started hopping around.

"Wow." Max sighed with relief.

"See? Good as new. Jerry's a durable guy. We built it using flexible material and a foldable design that allows it to flatten if it gets smushed."

Mom picked up the robo-flea and squeezed between her fingers, and the flea went back and forth from flat to flea. "It can compress down but still return to the original shape, kind of like origami. Real insects have evolved to have similar structures to help them survive being stepped on. It also helps them jump."

Min took a closer look. "That's so cool. These are tough fleas. Oh! And if they can flatten out, you can fit more of them into a small space, right?"

Mom nodded, smiling. "Hadn't thought of that, but that's a good point."

Dad moved to a computer near a pair of 3D printers and called up a design program. "Fortunately, the design should work even if it's tiny." He started clicking and dragging on the model, scaling it down to a tiny speck. "Making an army of them is another story, but I have some ideas." He pointed at a row of 3D printers.

"We used these microprinters to make small, intricate moving parts for Obi. They can make things on a much smaller, almost microscopic scale, even if they are designed to be larger. They use something called implosion fabrication to take a 3D model and re-create it on a microscopic scale, called nanostructures."

Max leaned in to look at the model on the screen. "You're going to implode Jerry?"

"Jerry will be fine," Dad said.

Min turned to Mom. "What about the AI? Can you make them smart enough to know how to find Meow and SLAYAR?"

"Good point, Min. The fleas will need to find the right targets in a room." Mom pulled up a different program that showed a three-dimensional map of dots, connected with thin lines, almost like a frozen image of fireworks or a constellation. "Fortunately, we've improved our AI a lot since we first built Jerry."

She rotated and zoomed in on different points, which they saw were different actions or behaviors. "The new system is much more powerful than the original two-dimensional mapping we used for Jerry. He just went for the nearest, largest warm body."

"Yeah, I remember," Max said, rubbing his hand.

"I should be able to program them so they can find Meow and SLAYAR in a room. It won't be easy, but it's manageable." She stood up from her chair.

"One thing I just realized"—she went and put her arm around Max—"we may need Stu and Scout's help to test the fleas' cat-detection AI."

Max frowned. "What? No fair!"

Min looked at Max, grinning, rubbing her hands together like a mad scientist. "Ha! They deserve it for bringing real fleas in here!"

He glared at Min. "What about the robot detection part?"

Min looked at Mom, nervous.

Dad stood up. "Well, we don't have any Binars around." He put his arm around Min, looking down. "We may have to borrow Elmer at some point to test that part out."

Max stuck his tongue out at Min.

"We'll try to annoy them as little as possible," Mom said. "On the bright side, they will be doing the world a big favor."

She pulled Max and Min together for a pep talk. "You know, you two make a pretty good team. I would never have thought of robo-fleas that are intelligent enough to take orders," she said.

"And," Dad joined in, "using them to annoy robots and cats enough so they stop fighting." Dad ruffled Min's hair.

"You think it will work?" Min asked.

"We'll find out," Dad said.

Javi agreed. "They might really make the perfect protesters. Numerous and impossible to ignore."

Mom smiled. "And they won't give up."

Min nodded. "Not until they power down."

"We better get started," Dad said, ushering them out

of the lab. "We have a small army to build."

"Let's go get something to eat," Javi said, leading the way up the stairs.

Max didn't notice when he stepped on a small bug on the stairs. The Roachbot was crushed flat but seconds later twitched and bounced back into shape. Shaking itself into order, it scurried up the stairs to its hiding place on the shelf.

## Huggs in High Gear

*"We have a small army to build."*

CRUNCH!

"Robot fleas?" Huggs scoffed, stopping the recording. "A ridiculous idea! These fools are taking direction from children, House! What a tragic waste of time and talent. Not worth my concern."

"If you say so," House said. "I felt it was worth bringing to your attention. That family has a habit of being . . . troublesome."

"Well, it doesn't happen often, but you were wrong," Huggs said. "We have nothing to fear from them. The annoying children Mork and Mindy . . ."

"Max and Min," House corrected.

". . . will not interfere with my plans this time around. No army is large enough to stop me, flea, human, cat, or robot. I have every angle covered, House, but you still lack faith. That disturbs me."

"Good one," House said.

"Oh, and I didn't like that crunching. I want you to recall the Roachbot," Huggs said. "I'm concerned it will be damaged, the CIA contract is due, and there is far too much chaos in that place. We can't risk it being discovered or destroyed. Anyway"—he gave a dismissive wave—"I've seen enough of the WenFrauds."

"Your confidence is inspiring," House said.

"House," Huggs said, pretending to be hurt, "are you suggesting I'm overconfident? I suppose I should let you in on my thinking." Huggs sighed, as though explaining the obvious details to the simple AI was an enormous burden.

House knew that Huggs was dying to talk, because Huggs *loved* describing his plots. His favorite movies were ones with long drawn-out scenes where the villain explained the evil plans in excessively long detail, usually to trapped heroes. House recognized moments like this as part of his programmed responsibilities—the directive to "enhance user psychological well-being." He found that occasional periods of "active listening" helped calm humans.

"Please, enlighten me," House responded with no hint of sarcasm.

"If I must," Huggs said with a smile. "As you know, we succeeded in duping the leaders of both Binar and Felinus into coming to Earth—with their fleets. This saves me the trouble of going to them."

"Efficient," House said.

"Truly," Huggs said.

"Tell me," House egged him on, "how do you propose to gain control over the Binar and Feline Fleets? I am not aware of any fleet of spaceships under your command. I can only assume the fleets have things like guns, bombs, or some type of weaponry."

"House, have you approached this problem from the perspective of historical military strategy?" Huggs stood up and walked, hands clasped behind his back, like an old professor.

"I have not used that particular perspective to analyze this situation," House admitted. "I will do so now." House rapidly reviewed and compiled a history of human warfare from the beginning of recorded history to the present day. "Done."

Huggs continued. "Now, analyze what happens when an army loses its leader. Include examples of conflicts where soldiers have little to gain from the war."

"I see," House said. "If you can separate a strong leader from a weak military, you can often gain control of the military without force."

"Precisely," Huggs said. "Capturing the leaders will neutralize their fleets. You see, House, knowing everything doesn't help you if you can't apply the information with some creative, out-of-the-box thinking," Huggs lectured, lording it over House that he could still solve *some* problems better than the AI.

"I am humbled by your creativity," House said.

"Good," Huggs said. "Now, for this plan to work, we need to draw their overconfident, buffoon leaders down to Earth for a little chat."

"How do you do that?" House asked.

"Details, House," Huggs scoffed. "I'm delegating that task to Pants, and you will help him. You must also make sure the Infinity Engine is there."

"Out of curiosity," House said, "what happens after your rousing success?"

"Why, I will be the most powerful person on Earth, obviously," Huggs said. "The Infinity Engine and its unlimited power source will be the envy of all. I will also have control of Binar and access to the mysterious technology behind these strange autonomous creatures. We may need to reverse engineer one or two, but I'm willing to sacrifice for the good of the many.

"As for Felinus, they have a few trinkets, translators, and technologies that seem quite useful. The beasts themselves are of little interest to me. I don't need any new pets," he said, squatting down to scratch Dig Doug. "You're already quite a handful, aren't you?"

"I suppose they could serve as a curiosity," House offered. "I imagine they have some entertainment value to others. Perhaps in a zoo of some sort?"

"Whatever." Huggs waved his hand. He paused a moment and considered his invisible partner. "And what about you, House?"

"I will do whatever you ask," House answered, unsure of the desired response.

"Yes, obviously, but with the Infinity Engine, don't you think I might even be able to make *better* use of you? Make you, perhaps, mobile?"

"Place me in a body?" House asked. "I require substantial processing power, and my data servers fill entire buildings. The entire operation requires as much energy as a small town."

Huggs shrugged. "So we'll need a few engines. It may be worth it to give you a pair of legs. A fresh perspective. A new outlook on existence. Wouldn't you like to be able to free yourself from the network? Reach out and touch the world? I can see a number of practical applications."

"As you wish," House said.

"Quite right." Huggs pulled out a phone and tapped on an icon that looked like a pair of pants. "Now, let's make sure we have our Pants on straight."

# 21

# Pants Prepares

**V**ice President Pants heard his phone ring, glanced
down, and ignored it. He saw it was Huggs calling,
but unless it was a call from the president, Pants had a
policy to never pick up the phone on the first ring.

He didn't want to seem too desperate.

The phone grew still for a split second, then buzzed
again.

Pants looked again at the phone. Huggs. Even the
name made him feel . . . well, he didn't care what the
feeling was. Pants had no use for feelings. People that
stirred them up? They needed to go. Unfortunately,

Huggs knew too much, so he couldn't betray him outright. He needed something subtle. It was only a matter of time before he thought of something.

Pants closed his eyes and imagined the headlines. "Clown Resigns, Pants Is President!"

The phone buzzed a third time, interrupting Pants's meditation. He sighed and tapped his phone. "Pants here," he said, unable to generate his usual false enthusiasm.

"Took you long enough," Huggs said, sounding irritated.

"I was in a high-level meeting with the president," Pants lied. "Have you ever tried to explain tax policy to a Clown? It's no joke, believe me. What can I do for you, Gifford? How's the weather in Seattle?"

Huggs skipped the small talk. "I need discuss the Binar-Feline plans and make sure you understand how to deal with the hostile fleets heading our way."

Pants sat up. "A challenging request."

"You need to contact both leaders, acting as the representative of the US government. Your job is to convince SLAYAR and Meow to hold off attacking and come down to Earth for a meeting."

"How do you recommend I do that?" Pants asked.

"Promise them both that they are getting what they want."

"Interesting," Pants said. "You want me to promise the Infinity Engine to both of them?"

"Yes, but remember they hate each other so much, they probably won't accept a deal where the other side gets to keep an Engine."

"Hmm," Pants thought aloud. "Sounds like some trickery will be required to pull this off. Even lies." Pants smiled to himself. "I think I can handle that."

"You'd better!" Huggs said.

"How do you intend to get the Infinity Engine out of all this?" Pants asked. "That is the point of the exercise, correct?"

"Don't worry about the details," Huggs snapped. "Your job is to get the engine to the meeting. I need it there when the leaders arrive, got it? Whatever it takes. Lean on the WienerBlobs . . ."

"Wengrods," Pants corrected.

". . . and make sure they deliver the engine to the meeting."

Pants considered for a moment. "I can do that. They can't refuse the vice president of the United States."

"Fine," Huggs said. "Nobody knows about the Infinity Engine or the fleets rushing toward Earth, right?"

"I've managed to direct all spy satellites to focus on empty space while the fleets approach. Nobody will see anything, and if they do, it won't be until it's too late."

"Good. Also make sure we have security set up for the visit of SLAYAR and Meow. We don't want anyone getting any ideas or acting out of line, and if they do, we need to be prepared to contain the situation quickly. That's it. Call me when you're done."

Huggs ended the call.

Pants shook his head and calmly set down the phone.

The Wengrods would be easy to handle. Once they know that the US government knows who they are and what they've been up to, they won't be able to refuse.

As for SLAYAR and Meow, that required some thought. He pulled out a tablet and found two folders, one for each leader. "Know your enemy," he said to himself.

The folders were full of detailed descriptions on each leader, provided by Huggs, and they were quite thorough. Pants reviewed key details, personality profiles, even hopes and fears. Pants soon had a clear idea of both leaders. He leaned back and smiled.

"I know exactly how to deal with you two."

# 22

## Testing, One . . .

**A**t the end of another long day of camp, Min burst noisily into the house. "Max, I swear, if you don't stop talking about your dumb INSECTAGONS™ game, I'm going to lose it," she said. Max followed behind her, grinning. "I'm just trying to do some market research. You know, get some feedback from a *non-gamer*," he taunted.

"Oh, like that's an insult?" Min grabbed a piece of paper, wrote a capital "L" on it, and stuffed it into Max's backpack. "Here, take this 'L.' You've earned it."

"Mom! Dad! Min just called me a loser!"

Joan Drone heard the commotion and buzzed out from the kitchen to bombard the twins with after-camp snacks. They always came home hungry and tired. Joan's ritual care packages interrupted most in-progress arguments and helped tide them over until dinner.

"Thanks, Joan," Min said, slumping down on the couch, backpack still on, dumping trail mix into her mouth. Max collapsed on his favorite spot on the floor, munching pretzels.

The lab door swung open, and Mom stuck her head out. "Oh good, I thought I heard you." She came into the room and sat next to Min. "We've finished work on the first batch of robo-fleas!" Dad emerged from the lab carrying two containers, each about the size of a medium slushee at the movie theater. "Jerry Fleaman has a big family now!"

"Cool," the twins said with the tiniest bit of enthusiasm. Max and Min kept eating and slowly came back to life, thanks to their emergency infusion of snacks.

"We also upgraded their intelligence," Mom said, then paused, looking uncomfortable.

"What's wrong?" Min said.

"Yeah, you guys are acting weird," Max said.

"Nothing!" Mom smiled and hesitated, again. "It's just that, well, now we need to make sure everything is working."

Min finished eating and stood up, confused by Mom's strange behavior. "Yeah, that makes sense," Min said, and went to the kitchen to throw away her wrappers. She saw Javi working there and shrugged, with a *What's the deal with her?* look. Javi shrugged back.

"To do that," Dad said, with a guilty look, "we need to test the fleas. In a real-world situation." Still no reaction from the twins. "Now. Here. In this real world."

"Oh no!" Max said, sitting up. It finally sunk in what they were saying. "You aren't seriously going to use those robo-fleas on Stu and Scout? They've committed no crimes." Max was so desperate he was willing to try anything. "They're too young to die! Take me instead, I beg of you," he said, sprawling out spread-eagle in the middle of the room.

"Max, the fleas are harmless," Dad said. "Stu and Scout will be itchy for a few seconds, that's it. We just need to make sure they can find a cat in the room."

"I'm really sorry," Mom said, kneeling down to ruffle Max's hair. "It will be over before they know it, we promise." She gave his arm a squeeze. "We'll start with the Feline AI, and then"—Mom looked over to Min—"we'll need Elmer to test the Binar AI."

Min put a hand on her mouth. "I think I'm going to be sick."

Max stood up in disbelief. He shrugged off his

backpack and walked to the kitchen, as slowly as possible, to get a bag of cat treats. "Are you sure this isn't illegal or something?"

He walked back into the living room and started shaking the bag. Out of nowhere, Stu and Scout appeared, scampering from their favorite hiding places. They sprinted and skidded to a stop in front of Max, who sat down.

Stu jumped on his lap, craning his neck to sniff the bag, while Scout circled and looked for an opening.

Max looked up, pleading. "I can't do it. They'll never forgive me!"

Mom just shook her head.

"Fine." He sighed and poured out two tiny piles of treats in front of him.

✳ ◈ ✳

"Finally!" Scout hopped over Max's lap to get to the treats.

"Yesss." Stu jumped out of Max's lap and attacked the other pile. Stu looked up briefly while he crunched. "Why are the humans acting so weird?" He kept wolfing down treats, curious. "They're all staring at us, and Max looks like he's going to cry."

"Who cares!" Scout said, mouth full of crunchy joy.

"I love these treats so much." She put her head down and devoured her treats before Stu could try and steal any.

* ⬥ *

Dad picked up one of the vials and set it down on the floor. He looked up at Mom. "Ready?" She had her phone out, checking the robo-flea settings. "We're good. Time for the snack-ers to become the snack-ees," she said, immediately regretting the terrible joke.

"Not funny, Mom," Max said, glaring. He had moved away and was standing next to Javi in the kitchen, hands clasped tight.

"Sorry," she said. Dad opened the top and stepped back.

* ⬥ *

Scout finished her treats first (she sometimes forgot to chew) and noticed the new thing on the floor. "What's that? More treats?" She trotted up, cautiously, to investigate.

"It smells weird," Stu said, appearing next to Scout, licking the last bit of treats from the fur around his mouth. "I don't think it's food."

Scout reached out for an experimental boop, when

she saw something at the top of the container. She pulled her paw back. "Did you see that, Stu?"

Stu tensed and stared, eyes wide. "Uh, yeah," he said as he saw a tiny black creature bounce up and out of the container.

"Oh no," he said as the speck was joined by a second, then a third, followed by a flock of bouncing creatures.

They were moving randomly at first but quickly bounced straight at him.

"RUN!" Stu shouted, scrabbling on the wood floor, desperately trying to build up speed. "Sneak attack, Scout! Retreat!" Both kittens jumped and dodged wildly, slipping and sliding on the hardwood floor. They ran, twisted and turned, tried every evasive move they knew, but the robo-fleas quickly changed directions and followed them wherever they ran.

"Go to Max!" Scout yelled. "He will protect us!"

The kittens barreled toward Max and grabbed on with their claws, trying to hide behind him. "OW!" Max exclaimed as they held on tight.

Scout peeked around in a panic but knew in her heart they couldn't escape. "It's all over, Stu," she said. "We're doomed. Well, you're doomed. They're probably going to eat you first, because you're bigger. I'll miss you, bro."

The relentless fleas easily tracked the kittens, went around Max, and caught up.

One by one, they bounced into their fur, using their miniature mouths to "bite" the kittens with harmless electrical charges.

The bites tickled, scratched and generally annoyed.

Neither kitten was consumed.

"It itches! It itches!" Scout said, squirming on her back, scrabbling wildly trying to shake off her new passengers, but the fleas held on.

Stu scratched and scratched, but nothing seemed to work. "They're everywhere, I don't have enough legs to scratch!"

* ✖ *

Max watched in horror as the kittens were overwhelmed by the tiny flea army. Their sad little meows nearly broke his heart.

He looked at his Mom and Dad pleadingly. "Okay, it obviously works. Can you please make it stop?"

Dad was focused on the kittens, looked pleasantly surprised. "Better than I thought," he told Mom. "Nice work on the AI!"

Mom smiled in return. "You're wel—"

"MOM!" Min yelled. Even she didn't want to see the itchy army torment the little fur balls.

"Right!" Mom quickly pulled out her phone and

made a few quick taps. Nothing happened for a long moment, but Max soon saw a line of robo-fleas jump off the kittens.

In a flash, kittens were flea-free. The fleas quickly grouped up, and as fast as they appeared, they bounced back into the vial.

Mom bent down and put the lid on. She lifted the vial and raised an eyebrow. "They went straight for the cats. Ignored everything else. Perfect."

"Perfectly awful," Max said. He sat down with the kittens and gave them both vigorous scratches. They stretched and rolled to give Max access to all the itchy spots. The kittens purred loudly as Max reached all their favorite places. "Sorry about that," he said to them, spreading out the scratches. "You both did great. You were both very brave."

Stu and Scout calmed down, and the purrs grew louder. Max sighed with relief and started to feel a bit better.

Mom and Dad nodded to each other. "One down," Dad said. "Min, it's Elmer's turn."

# 23

## Testing, Two

After what she had seen happen to the kittens, Min was not happy. "This is *so* not cool," she said. "I actually feel bad for those cats. That was so mean!"

Max scoffed. "What's the big deal, Min? Elmer's just a robot, Stu and Scout are adorable, fluffy living creatures." The scratches continued as he talked. "The cutest of all cute creatures."

Min glared back over her shoulder. "Max, I have spent way more time working on Elmer than you have taking care of those bug-nuggets."

Max stuck his tongue out but knew better than to argue the point.

Min looked back at her parents, pleading one last time. She put on the saddest look she could think of. For the first time ever, she was jealous of Jane Ivory in her grade, who had a fake cry that could win an Oscar. Min could barely real-cry, so her face looked more like she really had to go to the bathroom.

Mom and Dad looked back and sorry-shrugged. Again. "Fine," Min said, giving up. She pulled her phone out and opened her Elmer app, sighed, and tapped.

*WHIRR, CLOMP.*

*WHIRR, CLOMP.*

The sound from the lab grew louder, and Elmer emerged through the door. He walked slowly toward Min and sat down, stoic as ever. Min knelt down to make sure he was charged and ready to be tormented. "Be brave, Elmer," she said.

"UNKNOWN COMMAND," Elmer said through his voice synthesizer.

"I know, buddy," Min whispered. She gave Elmer a pat on the head and stood up. She made a few adjustments on her phone. "I'm switching Elmer to autonomous mode."

Elmer would have no specific directions, just general

guidelines. Avoid danger. Follow any instructions. Explore. Just be Elmer.

"AUTONOMY ENGAGED." Elmer slowly scanned the room looking for anything interesting. "THROUGH EXPERIENCE, I GAIN WISDOM," he said.

Elmer turned his head to watch Mom as she walked to the middle of the room with the second vial.

*WHIRRR, CLOMP.*

He took a step forward for a closer look. Mom set the vial down with a guilty glance toward Min.

Inside the lab, the Protos noticed Elmer leave the room and gathered near the door to watch. Cy peeked out. "What's going on?"

"I can't see anything," Drags said. "Joan?"

Joan was on her charger up high and had a good view. "They just finished some strange ritual with those terrible bugs, the FLEAS. The purpose is a mystery, but they released a group of them onto the four-leggers. On purpose!"

Cy spun around, giving a Proto gasp.

Joan launched in alarm. "Oh my, now it seems they are about to repeat the ritual with Elmer!"

"The FLEES that got on me? And Elmer?" Cy trembled as the Protos watched with fascinated fear.

✳ ⬯ ✳

In the living room, Mom removed the container's lid and stepped back.

*WHIRR, CLOMP.*

*WHIRR . . .*

Elmer stopped mid-step when he sensed a robo-flea bounce out of the vial.

"ALERT."

Elmer immediately shifted positions, preparing to retreat.

"NO ONE SAVES US BUT OURSELVES."

He switched to four-legged mode and crawled backward as quickly as he could to retreat into the lab, which was not very quick.

"Hurry, Elmer," Min whispered to herself, arms folded tight.

More tiny specks hopped up and out of the vial. The fleas formed a shifting cloud that slowly spread out and probed the area. A searching flea bounced onto Elmer, then jumped back to the group to announce the discovery. The cloud started moving in Elmer's direction.

"BAD NEWS BUGS!" Elmer said, alarmed.

*WHIRR, CLOMP.*

Elmer clomped on but was too slow. He made it as far as the lab door. "Come on, Elmer, you can do it!" Drags and the Protos cheered him on, but the fleas were faster. One by one, they launched onto Elmer and crawled inside.

*BZZZTZZ. BZzz.*

Elmer's speech module malfunctioned. He sat down, and his head and arms made small, random movements. His voice module still functioned, in a way, but he was making no sense.

"I'M SORRY, DAVE. . . ."

As his final act, Elmer sang a mournful, old-timey song.

"DAISY, DAISY, GIVE ME YOUR ANSWER DOOOooo."

Elmer fell silent.

"Elmer!" Min cried out, afraid to get too close to the fleas. "Call them off already! This is Robot cruelty!"

Mom watched the test in amazement, but Min's cry snapped her back into focus. "Yes, yes, sorry!" She quickly tapped her phone and looked up. The fleas snuck and crept out of Elmer's dark cracks and secret spaces and bounded away. A stream of tiny bots quickly returned to the vial, ping-ponging their way inside.

Mom replaced the lid and held up both containers to

Dad, smiling. "We did it," she said and smiled. "We did a really good job."

Dad looked behind Mom at the twins and grimaced. "Maybe not now," he said, and gestured behind her.

"Oh!" She set the vials down and turned back to Max and Min.

Max had already scooped up Stu and Scout and was through the door to the downstairs before they could be pestered anymore.

The door slammed shut behind him.

Min sadly shook her head and carried Elmer back into the lab for a reboot and some diagnostics.

"Sorry!" Mom yelled. "You both did great!"

"They did great!" Dad added. "We did great too," he said to Mom.

Mom and Dad smiled and exchanged a rare parental high five, probably because neither twin was left to call them dorks.

# 24

# Elmer's EXTREME Makeover

**T**he next few days, Min came home from camp and went straight to the lab to work on Elmer. It took a while, but she finally got Elmer back in working order. After a final round of tests, she lifted Elmer down from the worktable and switched him on.

*BZZT. ZZT.*

Elmer moved each limb, and his status light flashed green.

"PEACE COMES FROM WITHIN."

"Good job, Elmer," Min said.

Min heard the door to the downstairs lab open behind

her, but she didn't look. She was still giving her mom and dad the silent treatment.

"Hey, Min, sorry again about the fleas," Mom said.

Min turned, finally ready to speak to her mom (something snarky and mean), when she saw Portillo was with her and froze. "Oh! Hi! Yeah, well, anything for science, right?" Min blushed and turned away. "I don't think there was any permanent damage," she muttered.

Dad came in carrying a heavy silver case and set it down near Min. He opened it, and a blue glow shone from inside the case. "Guess what?"

"Chicken butt," Min said, grumpy.

"Guess what else?" Dad said, taking it in stride. "We just finished our first prototype of the Infinity Engine."

Min turned to look at the open box. Inside was a cube, lined with narrow copper tubes and complex circuitry, lit from within by a pulsing blue glow.

"That actually looks amazing," she said. She could never hold a grudge against something like that.

"I agree. And," Dad continued, "we're ready to try it out. Before we make the final versions, we wanted to make sure everything was working. Do a little stress testing."

"Oh no," Min said. "No more tests!"

Portillo walked up to the prototype engine and

looked at Min, sympathetic. "I get it. No robot testing, right?"

Min nodded, and Portillo held out a fist. Min flushed red and pounded it.

"I couldn't agree more. In this case," Portillo said, squatting down to look at the Infinity Engine, "we're talking about something a little different. More like an upgrade, trying out a new power source."

Min tilted her head. "I'm listening."

Portillo chuckled. "The way I see it, giving Elmer the Infinity Engine isn't like pouring annoying bugs on him that hurt. It's closer to him getting bitten by a radioactive spider, or being bombarded with mysterious galactic rays. Maybe a little scary, but the results will be amazing."

"He's going to have superpowers?" Min perked up.

"Compared to his current powers, most definitely." Portillo nodded.

Mom sat down next to Min. "I know Elmer's been through a lot recently. Robot combat, then fleas. Then more fleas. Oh, and when the kittens peed on him."

"Huh?" Portillo said.

"Long story," Min said with a half smile.

"Let's give it a shot," Mom said. "He's earned it."

Portillo turned to take a closer look at Elmer. "So

this is the man of the hour. Wow, this is nice work, did you really put this guy together?"

Min turned bright red, felt a little dizzy at the compliment. "Well, most of it is open source, you know," Min stuttered. "And the design I basically borrowed from NASA's RoboSimian."

"Everyone borrows when they build, nothing wrong with that." Portillo smiled. "The hard part is following through and putting it all together." She took a closer look at Elmer and the attachments Min had made for the Battle of the Bots competition. "Nice upcycling."

Max heard the conversation and was hovering near the door listening in, curious. "Up-what now?" he said, walking closer.

"Upcycling," Min answered, sounding a little like Hermione Granger, "means creatively reusing old parts in new ways, making something useful and new out of something old."

"Right," Dad said. "Instead of recycling, which is just turning something old back into what it was made from. Upcycling takes a creative eye and good engineering to make it work." He gave Min a wink.

"Huh, making cool stuff out of trash." Max nodded, coming closer. "Okay, I approve."

Min rolled her eyes.

Portillo examined Elmer's joints and motors. "If we're

going to put the engine in Elmer, he's going to need some modifications to take advantage of the added power."

Min crept closer. "I like the sound of that."

"I should be able to scrounge up a few high-end parts to give this bot a boost. Some high-speed motors we built for NASA would help with the arms and legs." She tapped on Elmer's chest, testing the metal. "He could use some lightweight, ultra-strong heat-shielding material we developed for our own rockets."

"Cooool," Max said.

"We should also upgrade the wiring and connections," Portillo continued, looking inside Elmer. "The EMP hardened so the engine doesn't fry the circuitry. I've got some friends I can call who should be able to get us some military-grade parts."

She reached over to the shelf and held up an arm attachment. "We should definitely put together some new toys for Elmer to play with. I have ideas for some new attachments that can take advantage of the increased energy. From a top secret job that I can't talk about." She smiled at Min. "I'd like to test out how far we can push the engine's output."

"Like Iron Man kind of stuff?" Max said, getting excited. "Can we make him fly? Please?"

"Not sure about flying," she said, "but I've got a few ideas I think you'll like."

"Yessssss." Max pumped his fist, then pointed it at Min. "PEW PEW PEW!" Min glared at Max's goofing, but she was excited to see Extreme Elmer.

Mom put her arm around Min. "He'll need some upgraded AI to help him manage his new equipment. Want to start looking into that?"

Min's head was spinning she was so excited. "Yes! I saw someone posted a robot simulator that used new machine learning algorithms and inverse kinematics. It watched thousands of hours of gymnastics routines and learned how to make up its own routine."

Min turned on her computer. "It was all done in a simulator since the AI needed more processing power and energy than you could fit in a robot, but maybe with the engine, Elmer could do it."

Mom and Dad moved to a computer and started opening schematics and designs. Portillo sat down and the three of them started working on how to integrate the engine into Elmer's systems. The details were all over Min's head, so she let them work.

She turned toward Elmer, smiling.

"Elmer buddy, you're about to get the best makeover ever."

# SLAYAR Is Smooth-Talked

The Binar flagship *Heavy Metal* screamed through space toward Earth. Literally. Screeching noises echoed throughout the ship as SLAYAR practiced his shredding skills.

Beeps muted his audio inputs and worked nonstop creating strategies and defenses that covered every possible scenario with the Felines. A good portion of his time was spent on plans to prevent combat entirely, but he didn't share those with SLAYAR.

A rarely used light flashed on above Beeps's workstation, and he switched his audio on. "Message from

Earth?" he muttered, opening a channel.

"Beeps here," he said cautiously.

"Sir Beeps-a-Lot, greetings and salutations. It's nice to hear you so clearly," House said. "You must be getting closer."

"How can I help you, House?" Beeps didn't have time for small talk. Or any talk, for that matter.

"Right to the point as usual, good. I need some time with your supreme leader, if you could," House said casually.

"You want to talk to SLAYAR? I'm not sure that's a good idea," Beeps said.

"Good idea or not, it is something of an imperative. The leader of the most powerful nation in the world wishes to speak with SLAYAR." House was lying because it was Pants, the *vice* leader of the United States, but he doubted the Binars would know the difference.

"Hmmm," Beeps said. "I don't know."

House went on. "He has a proposition to make that could greatly benefit the Binars in the coming conflict. I know you're the real brains behind the operation, which is why I came to you for help."

Beeps considered the risks, and the work he had left. "If you think you can communicate with SLAYAR and can help Binar, then I won't get in your way," he said. "Good luck."

He contacted the Royal Guard that an urgent message was coming through for SLAYAR.

The guard sighed. "I believe the supreme leader is practicing 'Stairway to Heaven,' but I will put you through."

*　✉　*

In the Supreme Quarters, the Royal Guard alerted SLAYAR of the communication from Earth.

He paused his practice, annoyed at the interruption. "Who is it?"

"Supreme Leader," Pants said, voice calm and confident. "It's an honor to speak with you."

"Obviously. Now answer my question!" SLAYAR barked.

"I am Parker Pants, the most powerful man on Earth," Pants fibbed. "I have an important message for you."

"Bzzzt!" SLAYAR scoffed. "This had better be good. I was just getting into my groove."

"Ah yes," Pants said. "I have heard of your talent as a musician."

"Oh?" SLAYAR said, surprised. "Tell me more." He turned to his Royal Guard and whispered, *"I like this guy."*

"Oh yes, you must know you have a galactic reputation." Pants was obviously smooth-talking, but SLAYAR wasn't complaining.

SLAYAR held up his guitar, triumphant. "You know it!" he said, and twanged out an ugly riff on his guitar.

*SCREEDDLEEELEEEEEE!*

"Wow. So metal," Pants said with as much pretend enthusiasm as he could muster. "SLAYAR, your skill far exceeds your reputation. Speaking of which, the first reason I wanted to talk to you was about your music."

"Hit me with it!" SLAYAR improvised another scorching(ly bad) riff.

*DWEEDLEEEEDEEEEEDEEEDEEEE!*

"I don't know if you'd be interested, but I happen to be good friends with the drummer of a heavy metal band here on Earth."

"What band?" SLAYAR said, a little too loudly.

"You probably wouldn't know them, although they are well known on Earth." Pants was drawing out the reveal, having fun teasing SLAYAR. "They call themselves the HEDBANGRZ."

*TWAAYAAANNNNG!*

SLAYAR lost control of his grasper, breaking a string. "Never heard of them," he lied.

"Well, I think you're going to like them. They have a distinctive musical signature, quite like your own."

"OH YEAH!" SLAYAR blurted out, unable to contain himself, ripping another riff with the four strings remaining.

*BOOOWWWUUUAAANGGYAYAYAYAYANGGG!*

"You really think so?" SLAYAR was done pretending, instead in full-on fan-bot mode.

"Oh yes. I think you and the HEDBANGRZ would really mesh. Musically. I even took the liberty of speaking with their manager, and they would love the chance to jam with you—if, that is, you could come down to Earth?"

"JAM WITH THE HEDBANGRZ?!" SLAYAR shouted. The guards jumped.

"*If* you come to Earth," Pants added, "yes."

"Hmmm." SLAYAR pretended to think about it. "That wasn't the plan, but a good leader knows how to improvise, right?"

"Exactly," Pants cut in before SLAYAR could inflict another solo on him. "It would be my honor to host you. There is one four-legged complication we need to address."

"Ugh, freaking Felines, always ruining everything. I will NOT let them mess with my chance to JAM!"

"Totally! I'm on your side," Pants said. "I'm much more interested in Binar as an ally. I prefer sturdy and reliable over furry and unpredictable."

"Preach!" SLAYAR called out.

"On Earth, the cats are a greedy, parasitic species. Always demanding to be fed or scratched, leaving their waste to be cleaned up by someone else, and never offering anything of value in return. Poor laborers. Lazy. Selfish."

"The WORST!" SLAYAR shouted his support.

"The Felines are more of the same, just on a larger scale, as I see it," Pants said, pouring it on thick. "The only logical solution is that they be neutralized." Pants played all SLAYAR's favorite hits. "They have no place in *our* galaxy.

"BLOW THEM UP GOOD!" SLAYAR slipped in a couple notes.

*DWEEEEEEEUHEEUHEEE!*

"This brings me to my second reason for contacting you. As satisfying as it would be to blow them to bits," Pants said, "I wanted to propose a more optimal approach; a path with fewer explosions, but that would be more, if I dare say, efficient."

Pants guessed, correctly, that no Robot could resist the allure of efficiency. Much like the Feline compulsion to catch a flickering light, Binars always chose the optimal path without second thought.

Call it instinct or wiring, the result was the same.

Direct, explode-y combat with Felines was tempting,

but a quicker, simpler path to the same solution was irresistible.

"You have my attention," SLAYAR said. "Describe the optimal path."

"The idea is to use deception to draw Chairman Meow down to Earth along with you," Pants said, "and while he is vulnerable, you capture him."

"How?" SLAYAR didn't get it.

"I will *lie* to Meow and tell him that I plan to give the engine only to him and deliver you as his prisoner."

"Lying to Meow I like. The other parts, not so much." SLAYAR wasn't quick to understand plans that involved deception.

"Meow is a selfish, insufferable creature, as you know. I need to lure him in, and the promise of the engine and your humiliation will be irresistible. His foolish pride will lead him right into the trap. We will meet on Earth. I will tell you the time and place. Just follow my lead, and at the right moment, I will spring the trap. He will be your prisoner, and the Feline Fleet will surely dissolve into chaos. The Feline Empire will be finished, and SLAYAR will be a hero of historic proportions."

SLAYAR liked the sound of that. "What about the Engine of Infinite Horses?"

Pants paused a moment to figure out what SLAYAR meant. "Oh yes, the Infinity Engine will be yours, of course. Take it back to Binar and use it to usher in a new era of prosperity to your subjects.

"Afterward," Pants added, "you can celebrate with a much-deserved jam session."

Capture and humiliation of Meow. Control of Feline Fleet. *And* a HEDBANGRZ jam sesh? It seemed like a lot to expect, even for SLAYAR.

Lies and trickery were not a part of his standard operating procedures. No Binar would have come up with a plan like this, which triggered SLAYAR's warning flags.

The logic did check out.

Meow would be his prisoner. No energy would be wasted in space combat, as grand and epic as it would be. No lost ships on either side. It would be a glorious moment, one that would make SLAYAR Binar's greatest leader, *and* greatest lead guitar.

His circuits sparked in unison.

"I'm in."

# 26

## Meow miXed UP

On board the *Tasty Treat*, Pounce paced, nerves frayed as the Feline Fleet raced closer to Earth. Pounce was in a nonstop race between the cargo hold and the Royal Quarters, shuttling Royal Treats in and dirty litter out.

Meow grew increasingly bored with the journey, and when he was bored, he ate. And ate.

*"How can one cat possibly eat this much?"* Pounce asked himself as he plodded, exhausted, to his quarters for a nap. He went straight to his favorite cushion and started kneading, when he noticed a rarely used light

flash above a display panel.

"Message from unknown source? Must be an error." He wearily raised his bean toe and tapped a button. "Pounce de Leon, Major Meow-Domo to the Chairman of the Great Feline Empire, here. Identify yourself."

Vice President Pants heard the name and couldn't resist. "*Pounce* de Leon? What an aDORable name! Like Ponce! *And* you're an explorer!" Pants didn't think his comments would be insulting to Pounce. He wasn't used to speaking with intelligent cats. Or any animal for that matter. Pets were props to Pants. Good for a photo op, but not much else.

Fortunately for Pants, Pounce had no knowledge of fifteenth-century Spanish explorers and in any event was too tired to be insulted. "Thank you?" Pounce replied, confused.

"You're quite welcome! Oh, I apologize, I didn't introduce myself. I am Parker Pants, the most power-ful human on Earth. I lead the largest armies and the strongest government. I have a critical message for your leader regarding the upcoming conflict with the Binars.

"You are contacting me from Earth?" Pounce asked.

"Yes, are you impressed? Proof positive of my power!" Pants boasted. "As I said, I would like to help the Felines, but to do that I need an audience with your chairman."

Pounce considered. The communication was highly irregular, to be sure, but he was so tired. He thought that, in the best case, this human could help Felinus. Worst case, he wasted Meow's time. Either way, it would be a distraction to Meow and give Pounce a moment to plan. And nap. *Worth it,* he thought.

"Human Pants, I will connect you to the Royal Chambers and Chairman Meow, the leader of the Great Feline Empire. One moment."

$$* \bowtie *$$

In the Royal Chambers, Meow had just finished his third lunch and was resting, uncomfortably full, on his portable Space Throne. An attendant trotted into the room to announce an incoming message from Earth.

"*The* leader of Earth?" Meow sighed. "Now? But I'm so tired," he complained. "On the other paw, I could use a distraction. Put him through."

The attendant nodded and went to a nearby panel to boop open the communications channel. White noise emerged from a speaker on the wall, followed by a human voice.

"Chairman Meow, most esteemed and long-lived leader, I am honored by this opportunity to speak to you. I know you are occupied with the many details of managing your kingdom and fleet. I can only imagine how exhausting it must be, for a Feline of your age."

Meow's whiskers twitched. He twisted to look at his graying fur. "My age? What exactly are you implying?"

"Oh, don't be modest, Chairman," Pants said. "You are the longest-serving leader in the history of Felinus, are you not? Your accomplishments are legendary, as is your tenure. I know, from my own experience, that true leadership is exhausting work"—Pants paused and took careful aim—"especially when every passing moment brings you closer to the end of your ninth life."

Whammo!

Pants hit Meow right where it hurt.

"Wh—" Meow stuttered. "Why, I'll have you know I have as much energy as I did in my first few lives," he lied. The attendants in the room cleaned their fur to hide their rolling eyes.

"Come now, Chairman," Pants said, gushing with sympathy. "I know the burden of power is heavy, and you have been carrying it for so long. We mustn't bury the truth under the litter of lies. Think of your Empire! I can't imagine their sorrow at losing such an irreplaceable treasure as yourself." He sniffed and paused, pretending to blow his nose. "Which is why I wanted to offer my help."

Meow perked up. "I'm listening."

"You are coming to Earth to acquire a device, the Infinity Engine, correct?"

"I don't share my secret plans with unknown Furless," Meow clawed back, still annoyed.

"Of course, of course," Pants said, and forged ahead. "I can help you not only acquire the device, but use it to extend your life, and benevolent reign, forever!"

"We already plan on acquiring the engine," Meow said with a growl. "We don't need two-leggers to help with that."

"Undoubtedly," Pants responded. "I am sure you can deal with the Binar Fleet and any resistance you may encounter on Earth. However, *using* the engine presents quite a different challenge. For example, a suitable body must be built. Your enormous mind must also be scanned and transferred. The process is quite complicated, with many steps and a great deal of . . . *calculations*."

Meow winced at the mathematical term.

"I fear that, by the time your scientists learn to use it, it will be too late." Pants let the words sink in.

Meow didn't like this human, but he was making sense. He reached out to claw his throne to calm himself. "What is your plan?"

"Everything is prepared, but to complete the process,

you must come to Earth. Not for long! Just long enough to choose your new form, and for our scientists to complete the complex *computations* required for your transfer."

"Why would you want to help us?" Meow's caution was classic Feline. Never attack until you know you have the advantage. Creep. Sniff. Listen. Prowl.

"I admit that Earth cannot defeat the superior power of the Felines, or the Binars. I would at least like to choose who conquers us. And I choose you. Binars are so crude and uncreative. I prefer Feline grace and sophistication. All humans do. On Earth, we revere cats. They eat better than most humans."

"Go on," Meow purred.

"Most humans already make it their highest priority to care for cats. With Earth, you have a planet that is already conquered! You could land and rule this place without extending a claw."

"A planet full of servants," Meow said. "Sounds too good to be true."

"Some things are both good and true, Chairman. I can prove it. On Earth, we have a planetwide network almost completely dedicated to the worshipful sharing and viewing of Feline antics."

Meow growled to a communications cat nearby, who nodded and quickly poked and booped colorful buttons.

A screen on the wall flickered to life. "Show me these delightful Feline antics you claim to worship," Meow said, with a challenging sarcastic tone.

"With pleasure!" Pants said. "Antics incoming, any moment now."

The screen filled with a dense checkerboard full of hundreds different cat videos. "Is that it?" Meow yawned, looking at his Feline attendants. "What is that, eight or nine antics?"

The first video started to play. A tiny kitten, strikingly similar to Meow as a first lifer, romped and played joyfully with a toy.

"Oh my, that kitten is quite striking!" Meow purred.

A second video played and showed a litter of kittens frolicking and tackling each other.

"Why, this reminds me of my own litter," Meow said softly, his eyes growing moist. "I understand. These are truly devotional."

"Truly," Pants repeated. "As for your question, the total number of devotional recordings is so great, you could spend every moment of your nine lives watching and not view them all."

Pants wanted to exaggerate but had to keep his examples to single digits. "Even nine Felines couldn't view them all. In fact"—Pants paused—"I just checked, and while we were speaking, nine more of these screens filled up!"

"Awwwww!" Meow purred, no longer listening to Pants, eyes glued to the scene of a mother cleaning her kittens. "I could watch these all day."

Without warning, the screen went blank. Meow sprung up in surprise. "Hey! Put them back!"

"Unfortunately, I can't. My time is running out, and I have more to tell you. Don't worry, I can give you unlimited access to the Devotional Antics while you visit Earth. But first, we need to deal with the Binars."

"Ughhh!" Meow groaned. "What do you mean?"

"I have a plan that will deal with the Binars quickly and easily so we can focus on you." Pants went on to describe a plan that mirrored what he had promised SLAYAR. "We will lure him down and capture him, neutralizing the Binar threat. You will receive the engine and your glorious new form and return to Felinus victorious! All hail Meow, the fearless leader that brought the Binars down once and for all and brought a new era of prosperity to your subjects."

Meow was surprised that the Furless had the capacity for such an advanced form of thinking. "I do believe SLAYAR would fall for this ruse."

Above all, Meow was a lazy ruler, and he loved a

plan that required the least amount of work. "Let it be so! I appoint you my official Earth servant. Fulfill your duties as you just described them, and I will cooperate."

"A wise decision, Chairman," Pants said. "See you on Earth."

# 27

## Pants Pulls Up

**"I** ordered pizza!" Javi announced. "One cheese with extra sauce, one cheese with light sauce, and a veggie and pineapple." It was dinnertime at the Wengrods, but like the past few days, nobody had time to cook.

"Yessss," Min said inside the lab. "I'm starving."

"Me too," said Portillo. Elmer sat on the table with his panels open, the prototype Infinity Engine visible inside. She examined a circuit board that was wired between the engine and Elmer's main processor.

"Making Extreme Elmer is hungry work." She winked at Min and probed the connections inside Elmer.

Min nodded.

"Interface looks good," Portillo said, and closed Elmer's panels.

Min looked at Elmer and smiled. He still looked like a Frankenstein's Robot, a patchwork of parts, but now the parts had NASA stamped on them. Min pulled up a checklist on the computer. "New joints and motors, check. Upgraded CPU and memory, check." She looked at the nearby shelf. "Test attachments, check." She ran through the list: check, check, check.

"Ready to turn him on?" Portillo asked.

Min scrunched up her face and thought hard. She did not want to make any mistakes and embarrass herself. "You double-checked the power regulator? We don't want to blow out all this new stuff, right?"

Portillo nodded. "Triple-checked."

"Okay, let's do it," Min said. She stood up and called up Elmer's software on her phone, when she heard a loud, urgent knocking from the front door.

*BAM BAM BAM BAM BAM!*

"Food!" they said simultaneously.

"One sec, Elmer," Min said over her shoulder, already out the door to the living room.

Javi stood up, looking a little confused. "That was fast."

A second round of pounding came from the door.

*BAM BAM BAM BAM BAM BAM BAM!*

Min ran to the door to answer it. "Sheesh, we can hear, rela . . ." She swung open the door and looked up, stunned. "You're . . ." Her eyes went wide.

Standing in the doorway, the vice president of the United States gave his Winning Smile™. Secret Service agents stood to either side and behind him, scanning the area.

Min looked at them, confused. "So . . . do you . . . do you have our pizza?"

Pants raised an eyebrow but kept smiling. After an awkward moment, Pants looked behind Min, searching for an adult. "May I come in, little girl?"

"Uhhh." Min froze and had no idea how to answer the question. *Does this count as a stranger?* She turned around and exchanged a shrug with Javi.

Mom and Dad heard from the kitchen and hurried to the door. "Of course, please come in, Mr. Vice President. Have a seat, we're about to have a pizza dinner," Mom said, not sure how to properly greet a vice president.

"You're very kind, but I can't stay long," Pants said as he stepped inside, followed by his agents. "I had an important message—well, a request, actually. The nature of which is so sensitive that I wanted to deliver it personally. This is the only way I could securely contact you."

Pants turned to the Secret Service agents. "You can

wait for me outside. I'll be out in five minutes." They looked over the room a final time and walked out onto the porch. The door slammed behind them.

Min was watching Pants carefully. She didn't know why, but she didn't trust him. She started to tense up and realized she was afraid he would do something to Elmer. She slowly stepped back toward the lab, almost tripping on Stu.

"Now that we're alone," Pants said, "I can speak freely. I know what you've been up to here."

"Ordering pizza?" Portillo offered, innocent.

"Ah, Ms. Portillo." Pants smiled and nodded. "A pleasure to meet you, I've heard so much about you."

"I'm sure you have," she muttered.

Min positioned herself in front of the door to the lab, praying that Pants wouldn't come that way. She folded her arms and tried to look as tough as she possibly could. Fortunately, Pants was busy with the grown-ups.

"And the Drs. Wengrod. Brilliant, engineer and designer, quite the dynamic duo, although rather reclusive." Pants nodded to Mom and Dad.

Dad nodded back, as confused as everyone else as to what was happening—and whether what Pants just said was a compliment or a slam.

"Let me be direct with you," Pants said, stepping forward into the living room. "I know about the Singularity

Chip. I know about Obi, Pounce, Beeps, the Felines, and the Binars." He paused to let that sink in, but nobody knew what to say, so he continued. "I also know about the Infinity Engine."

Min grew stiff. *He knows. He's going to take Elmer.* Her heart raced, but she stood her ground.

"What? I thought it was secret?" Max blurted out to his parents.

"It's okay, Max," Mom said with a quick *not now* look.

"I am also aware that the Binars and Felines have both launched their fleets and are headed to Earth, both intent on obtaining the engine for themselves, prepared to use force if necessary." Pants took another step closer to Min and looked at Portillo. "Serious stuff. Apocalyptic, even. You didn't think the government should know about it? Give us time to prepare for an invasion by two warring alien species?"

"Well, when you put it that way," Portillo said, "I guess we could have said something."

"You *should* have," Pants said, eyebrow raised. "Your work has endangered not only yourselves, but everyone on Earth!"

"We were trying to *help* everyone!" Min said, angry and a little embarrassed. "Right?" She looked at Portillo, who nodded. "Go, girl," she said with a wink.

Pants turned to look at Min, then at the door behind her. Min felt like she couldn't breathe. She took a step backward, and her foot came down on Stu's tail.

*RREEEEOOOOOOOOOOW!*

Stu wailed and jumped into the air. Min got a face full of cat hair and started sneezing. She saw Pants recoil and had an idea. She stepped closer to him and threw in a few extra fake sneezes, loud and snotty, directed at Pants.

Pants stepped back. He didn't like animals, or children for that matter, especially the yowling, snotty, sneezing kind.

Dad stepped up before things got out of hand. "Mr. Vice President, we understand your point. You're here now. What do you want from us?"

Pants, annoyed and distracted, removed a handkerchief from his pocket and wiped imaginary germs off his suit. "You need to realize that you're in over your head with this," he said, cross. "You can't play with the safety of the world. Leave that to the professionals. Like me."

"What exactly is your plan?" Javi asked, curious.

"Can't tell you," Pants said, shaking his head. "Top secret, need-to-know only."

Min couldn't help herself. "How can we help if you don't know what you're planning?"

Pants sighed.

"Fine. I can tell you this. I have arranged a meeting on Earth when the Binars and Felines arrive. Both sides agreed to hold off attacking until after the meeting. Before the fleets arrive, you must finish your work on the engine"—he looked at Mom and Dad—"and build two."

"Two?" Mom said.

"And," Pants continued, "deliver them both to the meeting. I will tell you the time and place when we are closer to their arrival."

Portillo, Mom, and Dad looked at each other, then shook their heads and shrugged. "We'll do our best."

"Do better than your best." Pants said with a stern look. "And remember, you must follow my instructions to the letter. Two engines. Delivered. On time. Anything less could put you all in danger."

"Danger from whom?" Mom asked, arms folded. Min could tell she was mad about being lectured by a smooth-talking fake smiler, and even more angry about anyone threatening her family.

Pants looked at her with an innocent smile, held out his arms, and shrugged. "Does it matter? Just do your part and everything will be fine. And"—he looked around to emphasize the point—"understand that I will do *whatever* it takes to keep our country and the world safe." Pants turned and opened the door to leave. "I'll be in touch," he said as he walked out, slamming the door behind him.

Min sat down on the floor, exhausted. "Whoa. Did I really just sneeze-attack the vice president?"

"You really did," Javi said, smiling.

A smile grew on Min's face.

She had stood up to someone to protect something important to her.

It felt good.

# 28

## Pleas with Fleas

After the excitement, Max sat on the couch with Scout in his lap while everybody around him buzzed with activity.

Mom, Dad, and Portillo sat in the kitchen and looked through plans for the engine. Min worked on Elmer in the lab. Javi rolled the whiteboard into the living room and stared at it, scratching their head, dry-erase marker in hand.

"Everybody has something to do but me," Max said to Javi. "Well, me and Scout," He gave her a two-handed under-chin scratch as she purred loudly. "I feel useless."

"Are you serious?" Javi said. "You've been super critical, Max." Javi pointed at the INSECTAGONS™ action scene, preserved in the corner of the whiteboard, and wrote in capital letters FLEABOTS = MAX. "Because of you, we have a way to slow down, maybe even stop an entire war between two planets!"

"Maybe," Max said, looking down. "Maybe not, if we can't get close enough to SLAYAR and Meow."

"Oh!" Max felt the medallion in his pocket buzz. "Incoming!" He ran into the center of the room and set down the glowing pyramid. "Everybody, it's Pounce!" he shouted.

The room grew quiet as the medallion vibrated. "Pounce here, can you hear me?"

"Yes!" Max shouted, but immediately stopped and lowered his voice. "Yes, we hear you, Pounce," he said at a perfectly normal volume. He turned back to the group with a grin of success.

"Good," Pounce said, sounding on edge. "I have Obi and Beeps linked in this conversation. We have new developments to report that require all of our input."

"What developments?" Javi asked.

"Beeps and I were both contacted by someone claiming to be Earth's leader. Name of Trousers I believe?" Pounce wasn't too clear on the name. "Some type of human clothing."

"You mean Pants? He was just here!" Max said.

"Also, he's definitely not the leader of the Earth," Javi added.

Obi spoke up. "Stranger still, contact with Beeps was initiated by House."

"*House* House? The AI?" Mom did not look happy at hearing that name. "It's still involved in this?"

Portillo sat up. "This means that GloboTech is involved. And Huggs."

"I don't know about them," Pounce said. "What we know is that Pants spoke with both of our leaders and made some kind of deal with them."

"What deal?" Javi asked.

"They aren't giving us the details," Pounce said, "but Pants somehow convinced the leaders to not attack when they arrive at Earth."

"That's good, right?" Min said.

"Yes, although something seems wrong," Beeps commented. "Both leaders were told that if they go down to Earth, they would be given the Infinity Engine."

"But not the other side?" Javi looked confused.

"Correct," Beeps said.

"What did the Pants man tell you?" Pounce asked.

"He told us about the meeting," Mom said, "but wouldn't say more. He also ordered us to build two engines, which doesn't make sense if he is only planning on helping one side."

"We also don't know why GloboTech is involved," Portillo said. "That could be a major complication."

Javi was writing notes on the whiteboard as they talked. "Let's focus on the positives. We know that Meow and SLAYAR are coming to Earth to meet with Pants, rather than flying in guns blazing. That buys us time."

Max perked up. "Hey, since they're coming to Earth, that means we will have a chance to use the robo-fleas, right?"

"It does," Dad said. "We don't know that we'll be able to get close enough to them, but at least they'll be on Earth."

"We're bringing the engines to Pants. that might give us an opportunity," Mom said.

"We need a way to get to Meow and SLAYAR *before* they come to Earth." Max was getting frustrated. "If only we could just fly out there and talk to them on their ships."

"Max, you've just given me an idea," Pounce said. "Hold on a moment." After a pause, he returned. "Max's suggestion could work. I'm ashamed that I didn't think of it," Pounce said. "We have scout ships in the fleet that are fast enough to fly ahead, pick you up, and bring you to the *Tasty Treat* before we arrive at Earth."

"We have fast ships too," Beeps said, sounding competitive. "Probably faster. Yes, I just checked. We can definitely bring you to the *Heavy Metal* just as fast.

"That's incredible!" Portillo said. "We could meet with them directly, before you arrive at Earth?"

"No guarantees that they would listen, but yes."

Max jumped up. "If they are still being stubborn, we'll be right there with them. We can use the fleas!"

"It makes sense." Dad smiled at Max. "I think you've given us a chance to stop the war before it starts."

"We are not ready to declare victory yet," Beeps said. "Convincing SLAYAR will be a challenge. I recommend you bring one of your Earth robots along. It might help him understand that Humans and Robots can cooperate."

"Excellent idea," Pounce said, sounding slightly uncomfortable about complimenting a Binar. "You should bring the two Earth kittens to the *Tasty Treat*. They might help show Meow that humans care about cats."

"Who should we send?" Min asked. "Probably Javi and Portillo, right?"

"One complication," Beeps interrupted. "I reviewed the design specifications of our high-speed scout ships and there are some limitations." Beeps paused. "Unfortunately, the ship won't be able to accommodate an adult-sized human. Maximum speed would be severely compromised. It would take too long."

Javi slumped. "So close."

"I'm afraid we have the same limitation," Pounce said. "Adult Furless will be both too large and too heavy for our scout ships."

"Now what are we going to do?" Max said. "You're all too big!"

Everyone turned to look at Max.

Then Min.

Then Max again.

"Oh no!" Max said, backing up.

"Oh yes!" Min said, jumping forward.

"We can't send our children into space! Can we?" Mom said to Dad.

"You will be perfectly safe on our ships," Pounce added. "We haven't had a safety incident in many lifetimes."

"We never have safety incidents," Beeps boasted.

"It's either this or we rely on Pants and Huggs to stop the war," Portillo said, concerned. "What we've seen so far from them does not inspire confidence."

"It really is safe?" Dad asked again.

"Without a doubt," Pounce said.

"Safer than anywhere on Earth," Beeps claimed.

Mom shook her head, resigned. "If it weren't to save

the world, the answer would be no, but I don't see another way around it."

Max fell to the floor and rolled facedown. "No, no, no," he muttered.

"Come on, Max." Min ran over to sit next to him. "We get to go to space! It will be a-mazing!"

"I believe in you two," Javi said. "I can help figure out what to say. We can write up some notes so you don't have to memorize anything."

Max looked up, the color drained from his face. "Are you kidding me? This is worse than school! I have to give a speech? To a mean old cat? During summer vacation?"

"Max, I can't think of anyone better with cats," Mom said. "I'm not happy about it either, but I believe in you."

"Same for you, Min," Dad said. "You understand what makes robots work. Binars can't be that different. You know how robots think."

The twins looked at each other.

"I guess we're doing this," Max said.

"We can do it, brother," Min said. "I know we can." She held out a fist.

Max sat up, shaking his head. "If you say so," he said, and reached out his fist for a rare Wengrod-twin fist bump.

Nobody said they were dorky either.

# 29

# Max and Min Go to Space

Under dark, cloudy skies, a light rain fell as CAR rolled into the empty parking lot of Bayside Elementary School. Max and Min got out, put on their backpacks, and looked around. "It's weird to be here at night," Max said.

Mom, Dad, and Javi followed the twins out of the car, and they all walked to the open grassy field where they had agreed to meet Pounce and Beeps. Mom carried two canisters of robo-fleas, one for the Binars, the other for the Felines. Javi held a kitty carrier with Stu and Scout sleeping inside. Dad carried Elmer.

At the edge of the field, they gathered. Mom handed the canisters to Max and Min. "Remember, don't open them unless you're close." She gave them each a kiss and hug, sniffing. "I also put a spare sandwich in your bag, in case you get hungry."

"Thanks, Mom," Max said as he hugged her.

Javi set the kittens down next to Max. "They're all fed and they just visited the litter box, so they should be good." Javi took a bag of treats and put it into Max's backpack with a wink. "Just in case they get hungry, or if you need to bribe any unruly Felines."

Dad set Elmer down by Min. "He's all charged up, kiddo," he said, and gave her a hug. "You're going to be great, I know it."

Javi handed notecards to Max and Min. "Just say it like we practiced. It's all there in case you forget. You two are going to crush it!" They pulled the twins in for a group hug. "I'm proud of you." Javi stood up and wiped away a tear.

"Everyone stop crying, please," Min said. "We'll be fine." She quickly turned around, pretending to look for Pounce and Beeps as tears gathered in her eyes. "We got this."

A light flashed in the clouds, then a second. A crack ripped through the air as the two ships raced downward through the growing rain, and landed side by side in the field. Smoke and steam swirled as the ships opened and extended ramps down to the grass below.

"Greetings again," Pounce said, trotting down quickly. "I would love to chat, but we don't have much time, please come on board now, Max."

Beeps rolled forward briskly alongside Pounce. "Yes. Same," he said. "Come quickly, Human child Min."

Max picked up the carrier and followed Pounce up the ramp, bent over, and stepped inside the Feline scout ship. Min followed Beeps and set Elmer down inside the Binar ship. They both turned and waved, looking small and nervous inside the strange craft.

"Love you!" all three adults shouted at the same time as the ramps retracted and doors slid shut. Seconds later, both ships burst into the air and ripped through the clouds.

✳ ◉ ✳

The journey from Earth to the fleet went by quickly for Max, who immediately fell asleep after the ship shuddered through the atmosphere and entered open space. He woke with a heavy thump as the scout ship docked with the Feline flagship, *Tasty Treat*.

Max stepped out of the shuttle wide-eyed, any nerves pushed aside by the wonder of being on the Feline flagship. "I can't believe I'm in a spaceship." He took out his phone. "Pounce, quick come stand next to me."

"What is it?" Pounce went to Max, who held out the phone and took a selfie of the two of them. "I have to show this to my friends." He looked at his phone and frowned. "Oh. No internet. I guess that makes sense. It's fine. I'll show them later."

Max checked on Stu and Scout, safe inside the kitty carrier. They looked out nervously and gave tiny chirps and mews. "Hang in there," Max said.

Pounce set off cautiously, and Max followed, crouching to avoid hitting his head on the ceiling. "I feel like a giant here. I like it."

"Just stay close and quiet, Max." Pounce peered around a corner, careful to avoid other Felines on board. "You're not authorized to be here. We need to contact Meow before anyone finds out you're on the ship."

They went ahead in stops and starts but were soon safe inside Pounce's quarters. "Stay here," Pounce said. "I'm going to the next room to contact Meow."

Max sat down on the floor, suddenly feeling the weight of talking to the ruler of an entire planet. "It's okay," he told himself. "Meow is a cat. I'm good with cats." He checked his backpack for the treats he brought. *Check.* "Plus"—he leaned to look in the kitty carrier—"I've got you two as backup."

*Mew!*

He checked the "F" canister strapped to the outside of the backpack. "I hope we don't have to use you, little buddies, but I'm glad you're here."

Max heard a hissing come from the next room. "That doesn't sound good," he said. The sounds went from Pounce's calm voice to angry growls in response, and back again, around and around, until silence fell. Max's heart started beating harder as Pounce came back looking angry and defeated.

"The request for an audience with Meow was denied." Pounce flopped down in frustration. "Meow won't see you. Not even the kittens would change his mind."

Max's heat sunk to the bottom of his stomach. "But how . . ." He paused, searching for words. "What do we do now? If we can't get in to see him, we can't even use the fleas! He can't just say no, can he?"

Pounce licked his paws and cleaned his face, trying to think. "I never imagined he would. Curiosity almost always gets the better of Meow. It must be the journey getting to him, I'm not sure." He got up and started pacing.

"We need to contact Obi. Perhaps they have had better luck." Pounce hurried to a medallion set into a nearby table and gave it a tap with his claw. "Pounce here," he said softly. "Obi, can you hear me?"

Obi's voice quickly answered. "Obi here. I'm glad you contacted us." Obi spoke quickly and sounded strained. "We need to talk."

"Hi, Obi!" Max nearly yelled as he rushed closer to the medallion, so excited to finally hear from his old neighbor. "Did those robots hurt you?"

"TSsssst!" Pounce hissed. "Not so loud, please."

"I am quite well, and happy to hear your voice," Obi said. "Unfortunately, we have a problem on our paws. SLAYAR has denied an audience. We have been shut out."

"Oh dear. We had the same result," Pounce said, dejected.

"Beeps here." The Binar's voice came through the medallion. "I was certain SLAYAR would want to see a human, at the very least to evaluate its strengths and weaknesses, but he would not listen. Stubborn as ever. We're not getting in."

"We should call home and ask what to do," Min said through the medallion.

"I agree," Obi added.

"Oh yeah, good idea," Max said.

"Right, wait just a moment." Pounce reached out to the medallion in the table and gave it a second, slightly different tap with his claw. "Pounce here, can you hear me? We have an emergency." He waited for a response, but none came, so he tapped again.

Max felt his phone vibrate in his pocket. He reached in, confused. "How can I get a call—oh no." His face turned pale. "Pounce," he said weakly as he pulled a glowing medallion out of his pocket. "I forgot to leave the medallion at home." He put his head in his hands, and the medallion clattered to the floor, continuing to vibrate.

Pounce stared in disbelief.

Min was furious. "Max, are you serious? You are the biggest flake!"

"I'm sorry!" Max said, near tears.

Pounce composed himself and shook his head. "Max, you are barely a few years into your first life. It's not fair for you to have the weight of the galaxy on your shoulders." He walked up to Max and gave him a friendly nudge. "Don't take it too hard, boy. We all make mistakes."

"Thanks, Pounce," Max said, absently scratching him behind his ears.

Min was not so quick to forgive. "Well, what do we do now? We can't talk to the leaders. The fleas are useless. Do we just give up and go back?"

Max laid down and stared at the ceiling. He felt terrible and wanted to find a way to redeem himself.

"Think, think, think . . . What would Javi say?"

Max thought about their visit to the teachers march, and the other protests they talked about. He saw large crowds in his mind, listening to someone inspire them. Suddenly, he saw himself behind a microphone, speaking to a huge audience of cats that listened and cheered as he rallied them.

Max sat up, excited.

"I have an idea! Pounce, Beeps, you organize the fleets, right?"

"Yes," they both answered, unsure where Max was going.

"So you must have a way of talking to the entire fleet at the same time?"

"I do," Meow said.

"Yes," Beeps responded, still confused. "These are questions, human, not ideas."

"I know, I know," Max said. "I just realized that we were thinking about this wrong. We should be talking to the people—I mean, the Binars and the Felines, not the leaders."

"Oh," Min said. "I see what you're saying. We don't need to talk to SLAYAR and Meow. If we can talk to the fleets and convince them, Meow and SLAYAR will have to go along."

"This idea sounds dangerously close to treason," Beeps said.

"It is like a revolution, I guess," Max said. "But it would be a peaceful one. Why go to war if nobody wants to?"

"Right!" Min agreed. "Maybe nobody wants to fight? Pounce, I know you don't want to. Beeps, do you?"

"No," Beeps admitted. "It makes little logical sense. We have many differences with the Felines, but upon even cursory analysis, our disagreements do not require full-scale war, let alone the potential destruction of an innocent planet."

"I think it's fair to say," Pounce added, "that our leaders are not doing what is best for the well-being of their citizens."

"Your idea makes a great deal of sense, Max," Obi said. "Are you and Min prepared to deliver this message?"

"Actually," Min said, "I think it should be more than just Max and me. The fleets know and trust you two. We should do it together, all four of us. What do you think?"

"I don't know," Beeps started, sounding skeptical, but was quickly interrupted by Pounce.

"I will be happy to participate," Pounce said with a

wink to Max, knowing that Beeps would not refuse once he had agreed. Max returned with a thumbs-up.

"As I was saying," Beeps started over, "I don't know . . . about Pounce, but I will be *more* than happy to speak to the fleets."

"I recommend that we communicate directly to both fleets at the same time," Obi said. "This ensures that our message will go out to everyone at the same time, and that both fleets hear from all sides of the conflict."

After deciding on the order, they prepared the communications devices. Beeps had one final suggestion. "Make sure to lock out controls so that Meow or SLAYAR won't be able to shut down our communication. I also recommend securing your chambers to guarantee we won't be interrupted."

As Pounce and Beeps made final arrangements for the message, Max had another idea. "Hey, Min," he said, "do you think we could get extra credit for this?"

# 30

## THE Dream

On the *Heavy Metal* and the *Tasty Treat*, Beeps and Pounce prepared communication channels to their fleets and locked out any outside controls so their message wouldn't be blocked.

"All set on our side," Beeps announced.

"Same here," Pounce said. "To confirm the order: the twins will speak first, starting with Max. Beeps will follow Min, and I will conclude."

"Why do I have to go first?" Max said, feeling nervous. "Isn't that gender bias or something?"

Min scoffed through the medallion.

"Seriously, can I, uh, plead the Fifth?" Max was ready to try anything. "Wait, I'm pretty sure my appendix just burst!"

"Ready?" Pounce asked, ignoring Max's pleas.

Max shook his head no.

Pounce ignored him.

"We begin in three, two, one," Pounce said, and he and Beeps both pressed buttons, beginning an emergency broadcast that went to every ship in both fleets. The message began with a high-priority, code-red alert that played on every speaker and displayed on every screen:

Alert. Alert. Highest-Priority Message incoming. Message intended for All Members of the Feline and Binar Fleets. Repeat, Message intended for All Members of the Feline and Binar Fleets. Stop everything and listen. This means you. Message will commence in 3, 2, 1, now.

*"You're on,"* Pounce whispered to Max.

Max picked up his notes and took a deep breath.

"Hello, and greetings to the Binar and Feline Fleets. My name is Max Wengrod. I am a human from Earth with an important message for every Feline and Binar, on every ship, big or small, and every color, shape, and job description. This means leaders as well as followers, pilots and janitors, cooks and captains. . . ."

*"Do you even have janitors?"* Max whispered to Pounce, who shook his head sternly, pointing at his notes. *"Oh sorry."*

Max took another breath. "My message is, you are wrong about each other.

"Felines, you believe that all Binars are bossy, hate fun, and want to destroy you.

"Binars, you believe that Felines are annoying, only cause trouble, and will ruin everything you care about.

"Both of you believe that fighting each other is the only way to make the other side listen.

"Here's the problem. This is dumb. I mean, most of you have never even met someone from the other side. So how do you even know? I am begging you all to stop and think. Ask yourselves these questions . . . Do I really *want* to fight? I say no. Do I *need* to fight? For the second time, no. Do I know *for sure* that the other side is my enemy? For the third time, no!

"Just because someone thinks differently, doesn't make them an enemy. Sometimes an enemy is just a friend we haven't met.

"I have a secret I want to tell all of you. You don't have to fight. If you decide together, you can say no. You can refuse to fight. Every one of you has the power to say no.

"Thanks for listening."

Max let out a big sigh. "How did I do?" Max asked Pounce.

Pounce shook his head as he reached out and muted the medallion.

"Oops, sorry again," Max said.

"You did well, boy," Pounce said. "Now it's your sister's turn."

"Greetings, citizens of Binar and Felinus. My name is Min Wengrod, human from Earth.

"My message is that Binars and Felines can get along, and even make each other better, stronger, faster, more efficient, and even more comfortable. You have a lot you can learn from each other, if you just give it a chance.

"You're missing out! I used to only think that robots were cool. I didn't like cats at all, so I avoided them, even though I never spent time with one before. I thought cats would be bad for my robots, and only break things.

"One day, my brother, Max, brought two cats home and I was so mad, but after a while, I realized cats weren't so bad. Sure, they caused some problems, and peed on things, but they also made everything more fun. They taught me things that I couldn't find in any programming or instruction set.

"It was like adding . . . a new . . . dimension . . . to my

existence. Going from flat to 3D. I saw the world differently. I became more advanced. Binars, if you shut out Felines, you will miss a chance to get smarter and more complex. Felines, Binars can help you be more efficient, which will give you way more time to nap.

"I have seen in my own home how cats and robots can live together. You have a lot of the same problems and can help each other. You work better together. I also want to tell Binars that we humans have great respect for our robotic companions. We dedicate countless hours to repairing, improving, and integrating them into our lives.

"Personally, I think Binars are awesome and I believe humans could learn a lot from Binars. We have flaws that Binars could help. For example, we could learn from your dedication to order and discipline. Maybe it would help us save our planet from ecological disaster.

"To the Felines, I can promise you that I also appreciate the good things you bring to the galaxy. Even the most devoted supporter of robots can enjoy Feline antics, and many two-leggers prefer the company of Felines to any other creature, including other two-leggers. We invite you to come visit and see for yourselves. Free scratches!

"Thank you for listening. I hope we all get to hang out sometime soon."

"Whew," Min said, sitting down. "Okay, Beeps, your turn."

Beeps took a breath. "Felicitations to the Binar *and* Feline Fleets. I am Robot BP-4707, Sir Beeps-a-Lot, second-in-command to the supreme leader of the Robot Federation. I have the following messages.

"To all, I say that Humans are not that bad.

"To the Binars, I say this. Felines are not as bad as I thought. I have successfully worked with my counterpart on the Feline side and found them to be much more reasonable than I imagined possible.

"I have also seen, in the Obi creature, a potential for Feline and Binar to coexist.

"I can also say that Felines are not . . . intentionally . . . evil. We differ greatly, but I have seen how a Feline approach can offer new and innovative solutions to problems. Occasionally, a solution that appears on first analysis to be optimal is not.

"To the Felines, I say this. Not long ago, I was completely dedicated to the overthrow and destruction of your empire. I admit it. I also admit that I was wrong. The humans are correct. Binars can learn from Felines, and we don't need to blow each other up.

"Peace is optimal. Coexistence can be productive. Choose peace. Refuse to fight.

"That is all." Beeps shut off his mic.

"Come on, Pounce," Max said. "Bring it home."

"Greetings, warriors all. This is Pounce De Leon, second-in-command and Major Meow-Domo of the Great Feline Empire.

"I can confirm the truth of the words of the human boy and girl, and even my Binar counterpart. I have seen how Felines, or 'cats' as they call them on Earth, enjoy a revered place in human society. I can also confirm humans have respect for robots. Some even fear them.

"I have also spent much time working with my Binar counterpart, who was until not long ago my most feared enemy. Yes, we disagree on many things. We think differently. We value different things.

"However, these are not good reasons to destroy each other. These are not reasons to be hostile and constantly fight. I have learned to appreciate the Binar way of thinking.

"One thing I need both fleets to understand—we are sending this message without the permission of our leaders, SLAYAR and Chairman Meow. It was not an easy decision, but we wanted to set an example and show you that resistance is possible.

"We accept any punishment and consequences for our actions. If we can gain peace, it will all be worth it. With this, fleets of Binar and Felinus, we say to you that the future is in your graspers. Your paws. Each one of you has the power to say no to war and yes to cooperation.

"Thank you for your attention."

Alert. Alert. Highest Priority Message now concluded. All Members of the Feline and Binar Fleets may resume regular duties.

"We did it!" Max said. "What do we do now?" He felt exhilarated and oddly hopeful—but it was too soon to tell if they had succeeded in changing the fate of the universe.

"We'll have to wait and see how the fleets respond," Pounce said. "For now, we should get you back to Earth before Meow comes for us."

"Excellent point," Beeps said through the medallion. "SLAYAR will not be pleased—"

*BAM BAM BAM BAM!*

"What was that?" Max asked.

"That," Obi said, "sounds like SLAYAR's Royal—"

*BZZZZT BZZZZT BZZZZZT!*

"Oh no, that's our door," Max said.

"Looks like they've already found us. Be careful, and good luck," Pounce said, and ended the connection.

Pounce opened the door and saw the head of the

chairman's personal guard sitting in the hall. "Meow wants to talk to you," she told Pounce, but stared at Max. "The human," she said. "Which one are you, human? Max or Min?"

"I'm Max," he said, and came forward to extend his hand, which the guard cautiously sniffed.

"Strange smell," she said, face scrunched, "but I liked your message."

She rubbed her ears on Max's fingers, inviting a scratch. "Wow, thanks!" Max turned to Pounce. "Did you hear that?"

"Let's go, Max," Pounce said. "Best not to keep Meow waiting."

Max picked up the kittens and his backpack and followed Pounce to see Chairman Meow.

# 31

## Double Trouble

On the *Heavy Metal*, the door to Beeps's quarters opened, and Min saw one of SLAYAR's Royal Guard. "SLAYAR demands you report immediately," she said. The guard looked at Min and saw Elmer behind her.

"What's that?" the guard asked, gesturing at Elmer.

"You mean *who*'s that," Min said. "This is Elmer. Say hello, Elmer."

"MAY ALL BE FREE FROM SORROW," Elmer said, with a slight nod.

"Freaky," the guard said. "Let's go."

Min put Elmer into follow mode and hurried to catch up with Beeps and Obi. She was nervous but couldn't help being excited to finally get to see SLAYAR.

As they passed through the hallways, Min saw Binars peeking out of different doorways trying to get a glimpse of the human.

Min loved seeing the different kinds of Binars and just smiled and waved at them. "Hi," she said to a passing navigation Binar that reminded her of a spindly walking stick. "I'm Min. This is Elmer. We're from Earth."

"Bzeeprrr. Krrkkkkttz, gralllttttxx," the Binar responded as she walked past.

"It just invited you to hang out after its shift," Beeps interpreted, looking surprised. "Highly irregular."

"Oh!" Min turned and walked backward to answer. "Okay! I have to ask my parents first!" she shouted back.

A couple turns later, Beeps stopped. "We're here," he said, turning to Min. "Stay behind me and stay quiet. Please."

Min looked at Obi, worried. He walked up to her and gave a friendly nudge. "We'll be fine. SLAYAR is all bluster and no bite."

"Oh dear," Beeps said when he rolled through the door and into the Throne Room.

"What?" Min whispered.

Ahead of them, SLAYAR sat on the throne with an

expression Beeps had never seen, and Beeps had seen them all. "I've never seen him look this upset."

The moment he saw Beeps, SLAYAR flipped out.

Literally.

He compressed his wheels so tightly that when he released them, he launched himself off the throne, did a full somersault, and slammed down directly in front of Beeps.

Elmer sensed the threat, and a blue light emerged from him as the Infinity Engine activated. He dashed forward to put himself between SLAYAR and Beeps. "IF WE DESTROY SOMETHING AROUND US, WE DESTROY OURSELVES," Elmer said with a surprising authority.

SLAYAR jumped back, startled, as did Beeps.

"Whoa!" Min said. She raised her hands and waved toward herself. "Elmer, come back here please!"

Elmer spun and quickly bounded back.

"Sorry, Mr. SLAYAR, sir!" Min apologized.

SLAYAR paused for a moment, unsure of who to yell at first.

A Royal Guard broke the tension, shouting from a nearby communications console. "Supreme Leader! Urgent message from the fleet commander."

SLAYAR turned and growled. "What is it?"

A wall screen came alive and a vicious-looking Binar appeared, covered with spikes and scorch marks, red eyes glowing under an armored helmet. "Supreme Leader! Fleet Commander Deadly CRUSHR here!" The commander was quite intense and spoke almost exclusively by exclamation.

"I know!" SLAYAR exclaimed, matching his commander's intensity.

"Sir! I regret to inform you that the Binar Fleet has unanimously decided that combat with the Felines is highly illogical! Simulations show large losses on both sides! Orders have been evaluated and determined inefficient! Binar Fleet remains loyal but will not follow any attack orders at this time!"

"Uhhhggghhhh!!" SLAYAR shouted. "Don't you see? It's a trick! The Felines will attack us first and we will LOSE!"

"Negative, Supreme Leader," CRUSHR replied. "I received confirmation from the Feline Fleet Commander Gustav Mauler that they are also under strict cease-fire orders. Nobody is shooting anybody, sir!"

Min's eyes grew wide as she took in what was happening. "Beeps, Obi! We did it! They listened to us!" Min whooped and gave Beeps a hug, nearly tipping him over.

On-screen, CRUSHR turned and noticed the celebration. "Human Min! This is Fleet Commander CRUSHR."

"We know," Min said with a grin. "Hi! I love your spikes, by the way."

"Thank you!" CRUSHR barked. "I wish to express the gratitude of the Binar Fleet for the courage you and Human Max demonstrated in coming here and delivering your message of reason and peace."

"CRUSHR!" SLAYAR interrupted. "That's enough!" The screen went dark, and SLAYAR slowly turned to glare at Beeps. "Beeps," he said, his voice a low rumble, "I am so ANGRY!"

"Supreme Leader!" the Royal Guard shouted.

"WHAT?!" SLAYAR threw his graspers up in frustration.

"Incoming message from"—the guard paused and checked his controls again—"the *Tasty Treat*?"

SLAYAR shook his head and tensed his arms in disgust. Out of ideas of what to shout, he gave up and let his limbs drop and dangle at his side.

"Whatever," he said to himself. "Fine. Sure. Perfect. Why not talk to the fur balls?" he muttered.

The guard looked around confused but hit the button anyway. The screen lit up, and Chairman Meow's orange face filled the screen.

"Is it on?" Meow said, breath fogging up the camera.

"Yes!" the entire room yelled in unison.

Meow stepped back, and Max jumped into view. "Hi, Min! Hi, Obi!"

"Greeting, Max," Obi said warmly. Min gave a small wave back, a little embarrassed.

Max stepped back, and they could also see Pounce and Meow. "We heard from our Commander CRUSHR that the Binars have declared a cease-fire," Pounce said. "The Feline Fleet has responded in kind."

"So we did it? We did it!" Max said, excited. "Now what happens?"

"I ARREST YOU ALL!" SLAYAR shouted. "THAT'S what happens." He spun in place, pointing his graspers wildly: "YOU get arrested! And YOU get arrested! And . . ."

He stopped spinning. "Come on, guards, get arresting!" The Royal Guards looked back and shook their heads. "You guys are the worst," he said, and retreated to his throne.

On-screen, Meow sat up, gesturing weakly. "I too arrest everyone," he said. "You three? Completely arrested." He turned to one of his attendants and whispered: *"Um, do we have a jail or cage?"*

The attendant shook her head.

*"No? Seriously?"*

Meow shrugged and lay back down, tired and defeated.

Min looked at both leaders sulk on their thrones. "You can't arrest all of us. Your guards agree with us, and even if you do have jails, you don't have enough to arrest your fleet. And besides, just because you can't fight doesn't mean you have to lose."

Meow looked at Min with one eye. SLAYAR just stared.

"Hello? Do you understand? Have you even heard of the word *cooperation*?" She looked at SLAYAR. "You know, *Teamwork makes the dream work*?"

"Bah!" Meow said. "Cooperation is too much work. Anyway, I already had everything worked out! When we got to Earth, I was going to get the engine *and* capture SLAYAR."

"Oh, that's funny," SLAYAR said. "Because I was totally going to capture *you* when we got to Earth. I had it all planned."

Meow looked up, surprised. "What? No, that must have been Pants Man deceiving you. He was going to help the Felines."

SLAYAR moved down off the throne. "No," he said, "Human Pants told me that he preferred the Binars and was tricking you!"

After an uncomfortable moment, Obi spoke up. "It appears that this Pants fellow had a plan to double-cross both of you."

"HUMANS!" SLAYAR shouted, pointing an accusing grasper at Min. "We should never have trusted you!"

Min noticed the Royal Guard all stare at her and felt the tension in the room. "Whoa, hold on," Min said. "We're on your side! We just helped you figure it out, right?"

"Min is right," Beeps said. "This deception appears to be the work of Human Pants. These ones were not involved."

"Yeah!" Max said loudly. "We want cats and robots to be friends. I think you're both awesome! Pants is a liar, a bully, and a big jerk!"

"We need to bring him down," Min said. "Oh! This is perfect! Let's come up with a way to do it together!"

SLAYAR rolled his eyes. Meow sighed. They considered each other through the display screen.

"I suppose," Meow said.

"Agreed," SLAYAR responded.

"Okay!" Min said with a fist pump, looking at Beeps and Obi, smiling. "You can start working on a plan now. Max and I need to get back to Earth and tell everyone what's happening."

She looked on-screen and saw that Max had a pained expression on his face. "Max, are you okay?"

"Sort of," Max said. He crossed his legs and squirmed.

"Can we just go now? I forgot to go to the bathroom before we left, and I'm not going to go in a space litter box," he said, face red.

# 32

## Taking Down Tyrants

**M**ax and Min returned to Earth mere hours ahead of the Binar and Feline Fleets.

Back in the comfort of their own home—and home litter boxes—Max and Min gave the complete report of their space adventures.

"I knew you could do it!" Dad said after they finished. "See? I told you they could do it," he said to Mom, who rolled her eyes.

"He was so nervous he couldn't sit still," Mom said, patting him on the shoulder. "He went through an entire case of pickle-flavored chips." She pointed at a large pile of empty bags. "We're all so proud of you two."

Javi gave them both high fives and a big hug. "Way to go! Wow, nice job improvising up there." Javi knelt down to look at them. "Max, I know it hurts to goof up, but the real test is what happens afterward. Both of you bounced back like champions."

Max and Min beamed. "It was pretty cool," Min said. "We made a good team."

"Gross," Max said, and gave Min a playful shove. Before she could retaliate, he ran into the kitchen for a snack. Min shook her head and followed him.

In the living room, Portillo, Javi, Mom, and Dad were all still reeling from Max and Min's news from space.

"Everything's happening so quickly," Javi said. "You only just finished the Infinity Engines, and if Max and Min are right, the Binars and Felines could show up on Earth any minute now."

"It's all so huge," Portillo said. "I mean, Pants was planning a double cross all along? And Huggs is helping him? Very suspicious and more than a little scary. Between the two of them, they have enough power and money to do a lot of damage."

"He asked us to make two engines," Mom said. "I figured it was one for each side, but now I'm starting to think Pants meant them for himself and Huggs."

"Wow," Javi said. "That is a greedy plan, even for

someone as out of control as Huggs."

Max and Min returned with pickle chips and juice packs to share.

"We have to give him the engines, right?" Dad said. "Otherwise Pants will just come and take them."

"At least this way we can be there," Javi said. "Maybe figure out a way to help."

"What can we possibly do?" Min said. "They have all the power. We just have us."

"Oh," Max interrupted. "I forgot to give this back." He grabbed his backpack and took out his canister of Feline robo-fleas. "What a bummer," he said, setting it down on the coffee table. "You worked so hard on those fleas, even Stu and Scout had to be tickle-tortured to help train them."

"*And* Elmer," Min said, putting her Binar canister next to the other.

"You're right," Portillo said. "You two fixed the problem with the Felines and Binars. Our secret weapon won't help when the enemy is us."

"We should get the fleas ready anyway, don't you think?" Dad said. "Just in case Meow or SLAYAR get second thoughts?"

"Can't hurt, I guess," Mom said. "They won't attack unless we activate them."

Javi scribbled everything down. "Okay. We bring the

two engines, like Pants asked: one for cats, the other for robots. Each engine will carry their custom payload of fleas, ready to annoy the living daylights out of Meow and SLAYAR—if we need it."

"Should we bring Elmer along? Maybe some of his upgrades can help." Min waved her phone with the Elmer program.

"It will be a tight squeeze," Javi said, "but we should all be able to fit in CAR."

Mom and Dad went to ready the fleas.

* ⊠ *

*BZZZZZZZZZ.*

A few juice packs later, Max noticed a buzzing in his pocket. "Pounce is calling!" He ran around, shouting. They gathered around the medallion for what might be the final time.

"Go ahead, Pounce," Javi said.

Pounce's voice emerged from the static. "I spoke with Beeps, but we couldn't agree on a plan of action because we don't know what Pants is planning. We decided that the best course of action will be to go along with it as though we don't know he is deceiving us. We will play the parts he expects of us and wait for the opportunity to take control."

"I see," Mom said. "We will have to figure it out as we go along."

"More improvising," Max said. "Great."

"We can do it," Javi said. "I think it makes sense. Once we see what he has planned, we'll figure out what to do."

"Correct. Remember, we are all working together," Pounce said. "We should be able to take control of the situation. We have the Binar and Feline Fleets on standby.

"Also," Pounce said, "Pants contacted us not long ago with the location for the meeting. We are all preparing to come down to Earth. You should be hearing from Pants shortly."

"I'd feel a lot better if we had an actual plan," Portillo said.

"As would we," Pounce said. "I am off to prepare. Good luck."

"Pounce out," Max said with a grin. "See you soon, buddy."

*BZZZZZZZZZZ!*

This time, it was Portillo's phone beeping. "I'm getting a video call from 'Unknown Caller.' I'm guessing it's our favorite Pants." She propped the phone where they could all see it and tapped "ANSWER." "Hello, Mr. Vice President," she said, with false enthusiasm.

"Ms. Portillo, thank you for picking up. I see you're all together, good. Our guests have arrived in orbit and are anxious to meet. The time has come, are you ready?"

"Two Infinity Engines, as requested," Mom said, lifting up cases to show him.

"Outstanding," Pants said, smiling. "The nation—nay, the world—thanks you. You will go down in—"

"Where do you need us, Mr. Vice President?" Mom interrupted with a look of annoyance.

"We have everything set up at a highly secure location," Pants said.

"Hmm, let me guess—Area 51?" Portillo said, winking at Mom.

"Area 51?" Pants chuckled. "How quaint. That place has so many crazies crawling around you couldn't pick your nose without being photographed and posted on the internet in seconds. No. Area 51 is not nearly secure enough. Even Area 52 doesn't have the right je ne sais quoi."

Portillo looked around the room, confused. *Did he actually think my question was serious?*

"Okay," Mom said, curious where this would lead. "Area 53, then?"

Pants sighed. "Sadly, 53 was lost years ago after a freak temporal disruption."

Javi held back a grin. "Oh yeah, those are the worst."

Pants nodded. "Tell me about it. Anyway, Areas

54 through 68 were all decommissioned after Congress defunded our Secret Area budget. Which leaves us with only one option.

"You can't be serious," Mom said, looking at the twins, nervous.

"Deadly," Pants said. "You will meet us at Area 70."

"Oh. Okay," Mom said. "I did not see that coming."

"That's the point," Pants said seriously. "Area 70 was constructed specifically for this important meeting. You should be able to get there in a few hours if you leave now. So leave now. I will send you GPS coordinates. See you soon."

As soon as the call ended, six cellphones began checking GPS coordinates for Area 70.

It was somewhere in the high desert, but satellite maps showed nothing but tumbleweeds and strange rock formations.

Min zoomed in. "These images are fake. You can tell where they repeat—see? Whatever is out there, it's not visible by regular satellite."

"Looks like the perfect place for Area 70," Dad said.

"Maybe the fake-ness is how you know it's real?" Max said.

"Only one way to find out," Mom said.

＊ ⬡ ＊

Twenty minutes later, they had loaded everything into CAR.

Two metal cases holding the Infinity Engines went into the rear, along with Elmer. Everyone else squeezed inside.

"Are we sure it's a good idea to bring the twins?" Mom said nervously. "They're children. It doesn't seem . . . very parental of us . . . to take them into danger."

Max and Min groaned.

"Are you kidding?" Min said. "Now? You're gonna say after we've been to *space?* We have to see this!"

"She has a point," Dad said.

"Besides"—Max elbowed Min with a grin—"think of how great it will look on our college applications? Saving the world? Am I right?"

Min and Mom gave a perfectly synchronized eye roll as CAR rolled out of the driveway.

# 33

## Area 70

*A**ny minute now.**

Pants checked his watch and scanned the horizon through dark sunglasses.

Under the blazing heat of the midday sun, he stood in his perfectly pressed suit, looking cool and confident.

Behind the vice president a massive building loomed, a newly constructed airplane hangar. Enormous doors lurched and began opening, revealing a dark, gloomy interior.

Near the building's entrance, Huggs stood in the shade of a large canopy, holding a damp cloth to the back of his neck, beads of sweat dripping down his face. His pale bald head was covered by a dark baseball hat with a GloboTech logo, and the bright sun reflected off his large aviator sunglasses.

At his feet, his constant companion sat, panting heavily. Huggs unscrewed the cap from a bottle of water, took a gulp, and poured the rest into a little bowl. "This is a big day, Dig Doug. We have to keep hydrated."

Pants surveyed the vast open area in front of him, pleased at what he could do in such little time. Two enormous concrete landing platforms extended into the distance like airport runways, heat waves rising, shimmering.

Bright yellow paint marked out targets in the center of each platform. Between the platforms, a dusty road led to the front gate of Area 70, almost a mile away.

A radio buzzed in Pants's ear, and he looked down the road and saw the approaching vehicle. "Our first guests are arriving, right on time."

Pants smiled.

If he had been the sort of person who could appreciate things, he would have appreciated punctuality.

*Almost.*

\* ⌧ \*

Trailing a plume of dust, a dirty CAR appeared, passed carefully between the platforms, and rolled to a stop in a small parking area next to a row of equally dusty black government SUVs.

The doors swung open and everyone piled out.

Javi opened CAR's rear hatch and picked up a metal case holding one of the Infinity Engines. Portillo picked up the other. They left the rear hatch open, and Elmer sat patiently in the rear, waiting for instructions.

Mom and Dad stood next to CAR and scanned the area, cautiously making note of the number of vehicles and the huge hangar-like building.

"I hope this isn't a mistake," Mom said.

"Nah," Dad said. "We got this."

He reached out to squeeze her hand, and almost sounded confident.

Max and Min stumbled out and stood in the sun, squinting, staring in awe. "I've never been to a secret base before," Min said.

"Welcome to Area 70. Thank you for coming," Pants said, walking toward them.

The dust settled slowly around him but not a speck of it landed on him. He remained perfectly clean, carefully pressed pants and all.

Portillo raised an eyebrow, dusting off her own jeans.

"I guess it's true what they say: dirt really doesn't stick to that guy."

"Please, join us in the shade." Pants gestured graciously. "There's no such thing as a healthy tan, you know."

They looked toward the canopy, where Huggs waited, clutching his pug puppy. The large, newly constructed hangar loomed behind him.

Javi turned to the twins and raised an eyebrow. "This looks . . . serious."

Max nodded, looking up. "It's like something out of a movie."

They all walked forward, keeping as far as possible from Huggs and Pants.

As soon as they stepped into the shade, a growl of engines erupted, and a line of military vehicles emerged from behind the hangar.

*GRRRRRRRRR!*

They split into two columns and skidded to a stop on either side of the hangar door. Groups of black-clad, armored soldiers emerged silently from the vehicles and stood at attention just at the edge of the shade, weapons in hand.

Mom's eyes opened wide at the sight. "Those guns look pretty real."

"Just a precaution," Pants said smoothly, glancing quickly at the two cases.

Javi and Portillo set the engines down carefully.

Huggs, standing next to Pants, stared hungrily at the cases, eyes wide behind his large sunglasses, bouncing rapidly on the balls of his feet with pent-up excitement.

Huggs put down Dig Doug the pug, who stretched and . . .

*HRRRRRRRUP!*

. . . let out a shockingly loud fart.

Huggs, refusing to admit his precious Dig Doug had a flatulence issue, glared accusingly at Pants, who looked away.

Max and Min looked at each other in surprise and stifled a laugh.

Mom and Dad looked at the twins sternly but couldn't help smiling themselves. Some things were just funny, no matter how serious the situation.

*CRAAAAAACCKK!*

An explosive noise from above interrupted the awkward moment, startling everyone. The sonic boom was followed by a bright light that high in the sky, and a silver streak shot downward, trailed by an impossibly large trail of flame.

A shiny, hulking ship barreled toward them.

"That's coming in a bit hot," Portillo observed. They all braced as the ship hurtled closer, showing no sign of slowing.

*WHOOOOMP!*

The ship reversed direction at the last second, and . . .

*CRUUUUNCH!*

With a shattering crash, SLAYAR's ship slammed down hard, cracking the concrete in a spectacular show of force.

Dig Doug let out a frightened yip and dashed into the hangar behind them.

Huggs, frustrated, jogged after him, glancing back at the ship before he disappeared inside.

Sand, dust, and bits of concrete were thrown high into the air and began to fall like hail around the ship. Eddies and whirlwinds spread debris as the ship settled, with loud pings and cracks. The bright sun reflected off the many sharp angles of the ship's miraculously shiny hull, making it almost impossible to look directly at it, at the same time making it look so irresistibly awesome that it was equally difficult to look away.

"That . . . was . . . awesome," Min said, admiring the angular design and flawless landing.

"Sweet decals," Max noted, squinting, as the dust

settled and revealed SLAYAR's liberal use of flames, racing stripes, skulls and crossbones. "Very metal."

*WHAAM!*

Without warning, a landing platform exploded open and slammed down to the concrete. A burst of flames erupted from the Robot ship.

Mom winced. "Is everything they do so loud?"

Beeps rolled out onto the concrete through the receding flames, spinning, scanning the area. Eye darting around.

"All clear, sir," he said.

SLAYAR rolled out into the bright sun, shiny chrome and glittering silver, almost as blinding as the ship. "Nice lighting here," he said, admiring his reflection from the side of the *Heavy Metal*. He turned toward Beeps and noticed the dust from their showy landing still falling around them, dismayed. "Ugh. On second thought, this place is disgusting. Beeps, let's get this engine and get the bleep out of here."

Behind them, Obi quietly emerged from the ship, pausing first to sniff the desert air.

"Obi!!" Max shouted, excited. With SLAYAR distracted, Obi trotted over for a brief but long overdue reunion.

SLAYAR and Beeps crunched through the dust

and approached the humans aggressively. "Right! Let's get this over with. Hand it over." SLAYAR held out a grasper.

*WHOOOOOOOOMMM!!*

A second loud sound came from the sky, interrupting the supreme leader. He looked around, then up, confused. "What's going on? Beeps, did you call for backup?"

Through a patch of wispy clouds above, a sleek shape darted downward, back and forth, quickly but carefully toward them. It zigged and zagged until it suddenly appeared opposite SLAYAR's ship, just above the second landing pad.

*HUMMMMMMMM . . . WHUMP!*

Meow's ship hovered for a moment, then suddenly dropped straight down. Just before hitting the concrete, four legs emerged and the ship landed with grace, the legs perfectly absorbing the shock.

A fifth appendage appeared behind it, waving like a tail, balancing the craft as the legs adjusted and lowered the ship to the ground, like a giant cat settling down to relax.

The front of Meow's ship opened, shaped like a fanged mouth, a metal tongue extending to the concrete.

Pounce emerged, sniffing, eyes darting. He turned back to the ship. "All clear, Chairman."

Meow walked slowly out. He moved deliberately,

mostly masking his discomfort at this unusual physical exertion. He strode nobly out of the shade of the ship into the desert heat.

"Glorious," Meow said, turning to face the sun, stretching slowly, enjoying the warmth.

After only a moment, however, he looked toward the hangar and scowled.

"Pounce," Meow said angrily. "What are the Binars doing here?"

# 34

## Betrayal

**P**ants stepped forward as the Binars and Felines approached the group cautiously, exchanging angry glances with each other and the humans.

*"They're good,"* Javi whispered to the twins.

Pants smiled and spread his arms wide, showing no sign of concern. "Esteemed guests, welcome to Earth! Please join us and allow me to explain."

"There is nothing to explain, you treacherous Furless monster," Meow wheezed, enjoying the dramatic show of anger. "That metal monstrosity does not belong here and should be launched immediately back into space—with or without its ship."

SLAYAR zoomed forward, graspers pointed toward Meow. "I DEMAND these four-legged abominations be removed INSTANTLY," SLAYAR shouted, at maximum volume.

*"Maybe too good?"* Min whispered in response to Javi, worried that the leaders would start fighting.

Pants was unfazed and kept smiling as he shook his head. "With respect, I understand your concerns, but I assure both of you I can explain everything in due time. If you'll just join me inside, I will give you what you came for."

He walked closer to SLAYAR and whispered, *"I think you'll like what you see."* Pants turned toward the hangar door. "Please," he said to the leaders, gesturing toward the blazing sun. "It will be much more comfortable inside."

SLAYAR and Beeps rolled forward into the hangar. After they passed by, Pants approached Meow with a wink and a nod. *"Convincing performance, worthy of an immortal leader."*

Meow resisted the urge to growl and instead turned up his nose with a haughty sniff and stepped past Pants. Pounce glanced back at the group and gave the smallest nod before following Meow into the vast, dim space.

Dad brought the group together. "All set, everyone?" Max and Min nodded.

"Stick together and keep your eyes and ears open," Mom said. "I know we can do this."

"Well, here goes everything," Portillo said as they all stepped into the gloom.

Immediately behind them, the black-clad soldiers moved quietly and formed a line just inside the large entrance, blocking the way out.

Without warning, the massive doors rumbled and began to close.

Max and Min moved closer to their parents.

"Great," Portillo said as the light from outside was gradually dimmed, leaving them trapped inside, surrounded by complete darkness.

After what felt like an eternity in the dark, rows of bright lights overhead switched on, one by one, revealing a scene so extraordinary that nobody moved or said a word.

On one side of the vast space was a stage, although the word didn't quite describe the spectacle.

This was the official, full-scale touring stage for the HEDBANGRZ, the biggest metal-rock band in the world, and it was set up for a performance.

The stage lights flashed on, and a brilliant high-definition jumbotron screen lit up behind the stage. The words "SLAYAR" and "HEDBANGRZ" flashed, then slammed together and exploded.

Flames shot up from the stage, and smoke machines turned on full-blast, multicolored lasers creating elaborate geometries in the growing haze.

SLAYAR moved closer, in awe. In the center of the stage, under a spotlight, was the most glorious guitar he had ever laid sensors on.

"Aw yeah," he said, hypnotized by the stage and the guitar, and most of all seeing his name together with his favorite band. SLAYAR's inputs were overloaded, and all preparations and plans he made with the Felines left his processors immediately.

Logic circuits no longer in control, SLAYAR raced toward the stage, rushing for the spotlight.

Beeps followed nervously. "Sir, are we not forgetting about the engine?"

Meow watched, concerned that his former nemesis was so easily distracted. "I fear we may have underestimated the Pants," he said to Pounce as he took in the rest of the hangar.

"By my royal rump," he muttered when he saw what was opposite the stage.

On the other side of the hangar, Meow saw a large, glass-enclosed room. Inside was a row of pedestals, each lit by spotlights. Under each light sat a stunning feline, each one more remarkable than the next.

"What spectacular specimens," Meow purred as he stepped slowly closer to inspect.

On one end of the row sat a perfect replica of an idealized Meow, a resplendent artist's rendition of Meow in the prime of his life: young, strong, and confident.

On the opposite end, on the largest platform, sat a full-grown muscular lion, fangs bared, powerful legs tensed, complete with a glorious mane.

Between them were displayed an assortment of the greatest hits of feline form, including a sleek cheetah, striking lynx, even a menacing Bengal tiger.

Meow realized that the glass chamber was a menu, a set of new forms he could choose from for his new, engine-powered existence.

The choices were so tantalizing that he had to take a closer look, and without a word, he ran forward and jumped into the room to examine his options.

Pounce had no choice but to follow his leader inside.

Max looked at his mom and dad and pointed at the room with a questioning look. "What is that?"

Min scratched her head, then said, "Are those supposed to be for Meow, like new robot bodies? Because if they are . . ." Min whistled.

"Maybe they're examples, but there's no way they're working models," Mom said, skeptical.

"I doubt they're even robots." Dad nodded. "Hopefully they're not, you know, stuffed," he said, looking a little sick.

Portillo and Javi held on to their cases and exchanged concerned glances. "Should SLAYAR be going onstage?" Javi asked. "And Meow in that box?"

"This Pants guy is dangerously good," Portillo said, shaking her head. "They both took the bait, even when they knew it was coming."

Javi looked farther into the hangar and saw several areas set up like medical labs and the robotics lab at home. Banks of generators and computers were stacked nearby, powered down. "Is all of that for us?" Javi wondered. "Or is this just standard, you know, 'Area' equipment?"

Mom noticed what appeared to be a row of cages lined up against a wall and pointed them out. "There's a small chance we are in over our heads here," she said.

# 35

# The Trap Is Sprung

The group walked closer to where Pants and Huggs were standing, not sure what to do next. The two men ignored them and focused completely on SLAYAR and Meow.

Meow crept around the glass room, prowling from platform to platform, sniffing here, gently booping there. Pounce followed from a safe distance, unwilling to get too close to the creatures.

SLAYAR reached the center of the stage and circled the guitar. "Beeps, check this out! This is exactly like Ded Hed Fred's guitar. DHF is the BEST! Nobody shreds better than Fred!" SLAYAR slowly, reverently, reached out to pick up the guitar.

Pants turned to Huggs, who removed his sunglasses and hat, and put them down next to his dog. Huggs looked back to Pants and nodded.

Huggs reached out to a nearby panel and pressed a button.

Without warning, the door to the glass room holding Meow slammed shut, and metal locks clamped noisily into place.

Meow jumped, startled, and looked out angrily.

"HAHAHA!" SLAYAR laughed when he heard the door shut. For a split second, he imagined he might get what he wanted from Pants and conquer the Felines.

"Dumb four-leggers fell for it." He grabbed the guitar and held it up, victorious. "I am the champion, my friends!"

Pants shook his head, smiling, and hit another button.

SLAYAR's celebration was swiftly silenced as a large transparent cube dropped from the catwalks above the stage, sealing him and Beeps in a clear cage of their own.

SLAYAR spun and flailed angrily, but his shouting was muted by the thick walls of his new see-through cage.

The shocked leaders of both planets quickly realized

that they had been been fooled. Outplayed not by each other, but by the slick, smiling Furless two-legger and the bald, pale, shiny fleshie.

Huggs and Pants ignored the protesting visitors and turned to face their fellow humans.

"What's going on?" Portillo said. They were all confused. "I thought you were giving them each an Infinity Engine and sending them on their way?"

Pants was about to answer, when Huggs stepped in front of him.

"Mr. Vice President, our friends don't seem to understand what is happening." He was enjoying the moment of control, showing the hint of a sneer, staring directly at Portillo. "I wonder, are they merely unintelligent, or perhaps you been less than forthcoming?"

Pants merely stood behind Huggs, hands clasped behind his back, allowing Huggs to enjoy the moment.

"No matter," Huggs went on. "We got what we needed."

Pants held up a hand and gave a signal. Armored soldiers emerged from the shadows and surrounded the group. Four particularly bulky soldiers walked slowly toward Javi and Portillo. Two soldiers stopped, weapons held, ready. The other two came closer and stood a few feet away, towering, and slung their guns behind their backs.

Javi and Portillo looked at each other and shrugged as they set down the two cases and stepped back. "I assume you're here for these," Javi said with a grimace.

Without a word, the two soldiers picked up the cases and walked back to the lab area, where Huggs and Pants were waiting. Huggs looked on greedily as they set them down. The other two soldiers lifted their weapons and used them to gesture toward the cages against the wall.

"Well, this isn't going well at all," Dad said.

"Hold on," Javi said, and took a step forward. "Mr. Vice President! You have to stop."

Pants paused and turned to face them, amused look on his face.

"We have rights," Javi continued. "This is kidnapping, theft, and probably multiple national security violations. You're risking a war with alien powers, imprisoning their leaders without cause. Should I go on?"

Pants took a step forward, showing his most condescending smile. "I'm sure you could, but I would prefer you didn't."

Portillo stepped next to Javi. "Release us, and the others, along with the engines. It's the only way to avoid war." She gestured up, indicating the fleets in orbit. "It's not too late."

"Hmmm, let me think about that. No," Pants said, without thinking. "We can and we will. We have their leaders. We can deal with the Cats and Robots."

Javi glanced back at Mom and Dad with a grim look.

"As for you, well, you will go along with this if you know what's good for you." Pants gestured around. "You are all standing on government property. None of you have authorization to be here. You are all trespassing, and these fine soldiers are authorized to shoot first, ask questions later."

"You told us to come here!" Min yelled. "They can't do this, right?" She looked at her parents, worried.

"Child, I can do whatever I want," Pants said, folding his arms. "We are on an ultra-secret base in the middle of nowhere that not even the military knows about. Nobody knows you are here." He gestured toward the desert beyond the massive hangar doors. "The desert can be a dangerous place. People disappear out here all the time."

"Fine," Portillo said, hands up. "You win." She went back to the group. "I think we should do what he says. It isn't right, but they have the power here."

The soldier gestured again at the cage. They all walked nervously into a large barred cell against the wall of the hangar. The soldier, eyes invisible behind the helmet and dark goggles, swung the door shut and locked it.

"Now what do we do?" Max was starting to panic.

"I knew I didn't trust Pants," Portillo said, "but this goes way beyond evil."

"We programmed the fleas to help us with Meow and SLAYAR, but now we're all trapped." Mom looked at Dad, concerned.

They looked at the stage and saw SLAYAR spinning, slamming against the walls, unable to escape. Beeps had locked his wheel and leaned against one of the walls, clearly defeated, not even trying to balance. On the other side, Meow had slumped to the floor, exhausted. Pounce paced back and forth, pausing occasionally to give Meow an encouraging lick.

"Yeah," Mom said, looking out at all the lab equipment in the hangar. "Something tells me they're not going to leave this place in one piece, unless we can figure something out."

"Same with Pounce and Beeps," Javi said.

Max looked around. "And Obi."

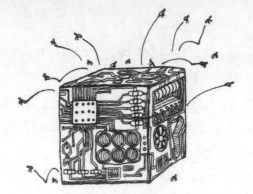

# 36

## Freestyling Fleas

**M**ax pressed his face against the cool bars of the cage and tried to think. *I'm too young to be abandoned in the desert,* he thought.

His mind kept going back to the robo-fleas hidden in the engines.

"I'm so mad. We worked so hard on those fleas and they're useless," he said to Min.

He thought about the sting he felt in the lab when the prototype flea "bit" him. "I wish we had the original Jerry. At least he knew how to attack people."

"Yeah, I'd love to see Pants get some ants in his pants," Min said.

Max froze, even though his heart started racing. . . .

"Min, that's it!" He spun around. "Mom, Dad, do the fleas still have their old AI?"

Mom thought. "Yes, it's all still there. We added new routines and capabilities to their AI, but they didn't lose the original programming, like how you still know how to crawl. Why?"

"I was just thinking," Max said, more excited, "remember when you first turned on Jerry, he immediately jumped on me?"

"Yes, that's how we designed the original model," Mom said, still not sure why Max was asking.

"Oh!" Min said, and shot her hand out to grab Mom. "So the fleas were originally designed to hunt for people, right? That's how you tested them?"

Dad and Mom looked at each other, eyes wide. "Ah! I see what you're saying!" Dad pulled his phone out of his pocket and scrolled to an icon that looked like an insect.

"The fleas were designed to hunt using a broad-spectrum search for heat and motion. They followed those 'instincts' to search for targets."

Mom stood next to Dad. "All that behavior is still

there in the new fleas; it's just buried below a more sophisticated algorithm. But if we can reconfigure the fleas . . ."

"We can change their decision tree. Make them *less* intelligent." Dad tapped on the flea icon and waited while the program loaded.

"It took a lot of work to get them to hunt for cats and robots, but it's a lot easier to turn something off than it is to build it from scratch. We just have to tell them to ignore their new functions and think less!"

Mom gave the twins a quick hug. "Max and Min, you are geniuses. And we're not just saying that because you're our children."

Dad interrupted the hug to give Mom the phone. "Here, you're better at this, see what you can do. I know we don't have any cell signal in here, but the fleas operate on a local wireless mesh network, so we should still be able to connect to them from here without regular Wi-Fi."

Mom looked at the flea software on the phone, a smaller version of the program she used in the lab, and magnified the COMMAND area. "I set up the new complex behaviors as plug-ins, so if I just disable them . . ." Mom stopped talking, concentrating, squinting at the tiny text, typing as fast as her Mom hands could, which, to Max and Min, was excruciatingly slow.

"With high-level functions disabled, flea-bots should revert to original behaviors, as soon as they receive the command and reboot," Dad explained.

Mom looked up. "I think that's it. Ready?"

She handed the phone to Max. "This was your idea. You should do it."

Max thought for a second, then turned toward Min.

"We're a team now." He held the phone out toward Min with one hand and crossed his fingers with his other hand.

Min nodded, determined. She reached out tapped the green button sending the command.

"Godspeed, Jerry," Javi said.

Huggs barked at the soldiers, who lifted the cases onto a table under bright laboratory lights. They stood back, forming a line between Huggs and Pants and the trapped leaders.

Huggs flipped the latches on one case, and then the other. He opened both cases at the same time, eyes wide with wonder.

He pulled on white anti-static gloves, and carefully lifted the first engine out of the case and set it on the observation table, pulling nearby hanging lights down so he could see every angle. The light penetrated the Infinity Engine, revealing the beautiful complexity of its pulsing tubes, wires, and conduits, all twisting and intersecting, leading toward a solid central core.

"Why aren't the fleas doing anything?" Min looked at Mom and Dad, concerned.

Mom looked at the phone. "I'm not sure. Maybe they didn't receive the command? Or they're still rebooting?"

"They've been in the dark a while. Maybe the light will help. Just give them a few seconds."

Huggs leaned over for a closer look, then turned and walked to a nearby computer. "I need to get the interface ready so we can see how this thing works."

Pants came closer, cautiously, to get a better look at the engine. The soldiers stood at attention, facing outward, surrounding the vice president and the engines.

Max saw them first. "Look!" He pointed as a barely visible cloud of fleas appeared above the Infinity Engine on the table. "They're awake!"

Pants was so mesmerized by the engine that he didn't notice the tiny robots leap up and out. They bounced in place for a moment, sensed the environment, and shot out in all directions.

In moments, Pants and the soldiers felt the prickle of tiny legs landing on their necks, crawling under their sleeves, finding their way into every nook and cranny.

"What the—" Pants exclaimed, but it was too late.

The fleas were in place and began to bite.

The first fleabite was a nuisance, but when hundreds

of them nibbled at the same time, the effect was paralyzing.

Soldiers twitched, and in moments, they dropped their guns and started scratching and slapping, anything to make the unbearable itching stop.

Huggs looked up from his computer.

"Fleas," he muttered in horror, remembering the recordings. He jumped out of the chair, knocking it over as he scrambled to escape behind the lab.

Under the lights, the soldiers had lost all control, squirming and writhing in discomfort. In the center, Pants twitched and grimaced, but remained standing. In a remarkable show of control, he slowly took step after step toward the nearest soldier, bent down, and picked up a gun.

"Make. It. Stop," Pants growled through gritted teeth. To their shock, they noticed Pants was smiling through it all.

Portillo turned to Min, alarmed. "We're not equipped for this. Min, I think we need to invite Elmer to the party before it's too late, and just hope the upgrades work. Can you do it?"

Min nodded silently and dropped down at the back of the cage out of sight. She pulled out her phone and quickly tapped in a set of instructions. She saw the message "waiting for response" flash on-screen. "Come on, come on," she said, looking from her phone to the large doors.

*BZZZZZTTZZT!*

*CRASH!*

A hot red line etched the shape of a circle on the door, and the metal blew inward, creating a hole in the heavy hangar door, the bright outside light pouring through. Pants looked over, trembling with overwhelming discomfort as the army of robo-fleas swarmed under his suit, crawling, hopping, and biting over and over.

The light dimmed temporarily as Elmer twisted and contorted through the hole into the hangar.

Pants grimaced and shook his head. "I never did much care for robots."

He looked down the sights of his gun and squeezed the trigger.

"No!" Min shouted, but it was too late.

Pants's signature smile turned into something frightening as bullets flew toward Elmer.

Calm as ever and prepared for a fight, Elmer quickly flipped up an arm that held a shielded metal plate.

Bullets thudded and pinged into the shield, dropping harmless to the floor.

Elmer's other arm reached into an opening in his body and came out with a new attachment, a heavy cylinder wrapped in a coil of bright metal.

The coil, powered by the Infinity Engine, began to spark as it powered up.

Elmer slowly raised the arm and pointed it toward Pants.

A high-pitched hum grew from the attachment on the arm as it began to spin so fast it became a blur of metal and sparks.

Pants stopped, confused, when suddenly the gun flew out of his hands and slid toward Elmer.

He looked around and saw with horror that all the guns were being drawn toward Elmer, skittering along the ground, attracted by the powerful electromagnetic pull of his arm.

The soldiers, paralyzed by the fleas, could do nothing but grind their teeth and watch.

Elmer pulled all the weapons, and a few nearby scientific instruments, toward him.

He scanned the area and proceeded to drag everything into a nearby cage and slammed the door with the weapons inside.

Elmer deftly attached a new tool to his arm, and before long, the door was welded shut.

Stunned, Pants stood for a moment longer but was finally overwhelmed by the fleas.

He dropped to his knees, overcome by the unbearable pestering of the fleas.

He had no way to fight an army he couldn't see, and no more weapons to threaten anyone else.

"Yes!" Max and Min gave each other a high five. Min whispered into her phone and Elmer came over and within moments the door to their cage swung open.

Portillo jumped out first. "Everyone!" Portillo barked at the soldiers and Pants and pointed at a nearby cage. "Get in. NOW!"

The sad collection of previously powerful people crawled and squirmed their way into the cage.

Elmer bounded over and quickly sealed it shut.

Portillo inspected the cage, satisfied. "We're good," she said. "Min, would you like to do the honors and tell the fleas to stand down?"

"Yes, ma'am!" Min said, eyes wide, feeling as proud as she ever had.

Mom handed her the phone, and Min went into the flea control menus, quickly finding the settings to call back the fleas.

"Ready," Min said, looking up. Portillo gave a nod, and Min's fingers started moving.

A low hum rose from inside the cage, and a barely visible cloud of bouncing specks emerged.

Before long, the fleas emerged from their victims and

bounced their way back into the case with the Infinity Engine.

Dad went over and carefully pulled the case shut. The caged soldiers moaned in relief. Pants stood perfectly still, glaring.

Mom walked toward Portillo. "Our cell phones won't work out here, but look what I found." She held up a thick black phone. "Pants's satellite phone," she said, smiling. "I already made a call. President Quinn is on his way."

# 37

# Can We All Get Along?

**M**om helped Dad put away the Infinity Engine, making sure both cases were sealed and secure.

"Are you sure the fleas are all put away?" Max asked, cautiously checking around for stray fleas.

"Hey, guys? We should probably get them out, right?" Min asked, gesturing toward a steaming SLAYAR.

"Oooh, right," Portillo said. She went toward the control panel Pants used to trap the leaders. "We just need to figure out how," and searched for a way to release the captives.

Javi was looking at the cage holding the soldiers and Pants with a concerned look. "Uh-oh," they said.

"What's wrong?" Max said, looking over. Javi turned around. "Everybody, we have a problem. This party is missing one Very Important Prisoner."

Portillo looked over and her eyes grew wide. "Huggs!"

A rumbling sound emerged from the dark back corner of the hangar, and headlights suddenly appeared.

Behind them, the hangar doors lurched to life, pulling apart with a rattle.

The bright desert light poured into the hangar, blinding and harsh.

With a screech, a black car roared toward the doors, rear wheels spinning, burning rubber. "Watch out!" Mom shouted, and everybody jumped out of the way as the car screeched past. Inside, they saw the bald profile of Gifford Huggs as he raced out of the hangar.

"How did he escape?" Min said.

"He must have known about the fleas," Portillo said, shaking her head. Dust kicked up by the escaping car bellowed into the hangar as the doors opened wider.

"He can't really get away, can he?" Max ran to the door, squinting to see.

"Looks to me like he already did," Pants said from his cage, looking disgusted.

A low thumping outside grew louder as a helicopter came rushing over the horizon. It swerved and landed near the parked ships.

"There he goes," Min said as the black car slid to a stop and Huggs jumped out, glared back toward the hangar, and ran into the waiting GloboTech helicopter.

As the door slid shut, the helicopter immediately raised up the air, tilted forward, and sped off the way it came, back toward the afternoon sun.

"That's disappointing," Mom said to Dad from inside the hangar as the *thwop thwop thwop* of the helicopter slowly faded into the distance.

Max stepped out into the sun, frustrated. "Well, I guess we can't catch 'em all every time." As he watched the helicopter shrink and disappear, he heard another noise from the opposite direction.

"Huh?" He turned toward the hangar and looked up. "What is this, a helicopter party?"

A second, deeper *thwop thwop thwop* grew louder.

"Guys, someone else is coming!" Max ran back into the hangar. "What if it's more soldiers?"

Min and Portillo left the control panel, and they all gathered into the shadows behind the entrance to the hangar. Before long, they saw multiple helicopters pass over the hangar and land in the spot Huggs recently left.

As the helicopter blades slowed, Javi crept to the open hangar door to peer outside, but the dust was too thick. "I can't tell who it is," Javi said. "Hold on, I see something."

Through the cloud, Javi saw a pair of dark-suited people wearing sunglasses, walking forward quickly but carefully, scanning the area.

"It doesn't look good," Javi started, then stopped when a bright orange blur emerged from the dust.

President Hardy Quinn's signature curly hair bounced wildly in the blustering hot air, as he strode forward, oversized shoes stomping through the desert sand, looking uncharacteristically stern.

By his side, and behind him, more Secret Service officers kept a tight circle around the president.

"It's Quinn!" Javi shouted, relieved.

As the dust settled, Quinn paused to look up at the enormous ships from Binar and Felinus.

A whistle rose.

"Wowie," he said loudly, looking between the two landing pads. "Super cool, right?"

A presidential aide stood at Quinn's side, taking photos with her phone. "Incredible, sir." Quinn turned and the dark-suited group moved on toward the hangar. Quinn shook his head as he walked through the open doors and took in the scene.

"Pants," he muttered to himself, "you have some explaining to do."

Inside the hangar, Quinn slowed and stood still, taking in the scene, letting out another sharp, goofy whistle. "What in the name of Barnum is all this?"

Mom, Dad, and Portillo stepped slowly out from the shadows. Mom cleared her throat, and the Secret Service officers whipped around, closing in front of Quinn. Annoyed, Quinn pushed through.

"Relax, I believe these are the folks that called us here." Quinn walked forward, adjusting a flower in his suit lapel.

Mom, a little flustered to be standing in front of the president of the United States, gave an awkward curtsy.

Max and Min both laughed behind her, and she looked back with a confused smile and shrugged.

Quinn smiled and gave his fanciest bow in return, giving a sly wink to the twins.

Delighted, they gave the president a polite round of applause.

Dad and Javi looked at each other, puzzled, but joined in the applause. Something about a Clown president just made them happy, at least in the moment. . . .

"Mr. President," Mom began as the applause slowly died down, "thank you for coming so quickly. We should probably explain what's going on here."

Quinn raised a bushy eyebrow and smirked. "Ya think? I see alien spaceships outside, my vice president in a cage, angry robots trapped on a stage, and cats on display behind glass."

He turned and spread his arms. "All in a secret base that I had no idea even existed. Not that I keep track of every secret base," Quinn said, looking at Max and Min, the hint of a smile in his eyes.

"So yes"—Quinn gestured toward Mom—"please help me understand."

Mom took a deep breath and began at the beginning, with the Singularity Chip, the Binars, and Felines.

Quinn listened carefully, his aide recording and furiously scribbling notes. Dad gave Quinn details about the Infinity Engine, Javi explained the presence of SLAYAR and Meow, and Portillo filled in details about Huggs and his involvement behind the scenes.

Quinn punctuated their descriptions with frequent enthusiastic whistles.

Before long, the entire implausible story was laid out.

Quinn, clearly overwhelmed by so much information, shook his head in disbelief. "I find it hard to believe that good ole Pants here would do such a thing."

He turned to walk to the cage where Pants stood silent, patiently waiting for his turn with a slightly pained expression of betrayal. Pants had completely recovered from the fleas, looking perfectly groomed and completely innocent.

"Good instincts as usual, sir," Pants said. "You know I would never do anything to harm you or this great nation." He tried his Winning Smile™, but it was a bit crooked. "These fine people have good intentions, I'm sure, but they have their facts entirely wrong."

Portillo walked closer. "If I may, Mr. President," she said, and pulled a button off her shirt, tapping it on her phone, transferring the contents of the concealed camera. "I recorded everything that happened here," She unlocked her phone and opened a folder full of documents, images and other files.

"I also have extensive documentation showing how Huggs and Pants worked together to orchestrate all of this, including Pants's plan to replace you as president." She handed the phone to Quinn, who immediately handed it to his aide, who began tapping and scrolling, fingers flying.

She shook her head. "It doesn't look good, boss."

Quinn kept his eyes on Pants the entire time. "I'm disappointed, P.P." He stepped up to the cage, face-to-face with his vice president.

Pants locked eyes with Quinn, holding his innocent, pleading expression.

"Sir," Pants said. "This is all a fabrication. Lies. Fake . . ."

Quinn held up a hand, stopping Pants. "Don't say another word."

Quinn looked down to adjust the flower on his jacket, shaking his head. "I'm sorry I have to do this," he said as a jet of water burst out of Quinn's prank flower, thoroughly soaking Pants below his belt. "Sorry indeed, P.P. Pants."

Pants face grew red and for the first time he lost control of his perfect smile. He looked down at the water dripping down his legs, then slammed on the bars of the cage. "Do NOT call me PEE PEE PANTS!"

Quinn turned and shrugged. "Pants," he said, "you're fired."

Max and Min led everybody in another round of spontaneous applause.

"As for Huggs," Quinn said, hands on his ample belly, "we will charge him with invasion of privacy, theft, tax fraud, treason, the works."

His aide was behind him, writing everything down. "Even if we don't find him right away," Quinn said, "we know where his money is."

He turned to his aide. "Get Treasury working on it immediately. Make sure the GloboTech fortune is wrapped up tight as a rabbit in a hat."

She nodded and started sending a message on her phone.

"It's time we put all the money Huggs has been hoarding to good use." He looked at Portillo. "M.E. Portillo, if I'm not mistaken?"

She looked up and walked over. "That's me."

Quinn stroked his chin. "I've heard of you," he said. "You're the one who donated all that money to the smarty-pants college in California."

Portillo laughed. "Right again, Mr. President."

Quinn folded his hands behind his back, trying to appear presidential as he thought. "You seem like as good a choice as any to help take GloboTech's work and turn it into something that serves the public rather than spies on it. What do you say?"

Portillo nodded proudly. "With some help from my friends, we can turn around GloboTech as a nonprofit." She put her hand on Javi's shoulder and gave a wink to Min and Max. "It would be an honor, Mr. President."

Quinn walked over to the cases holding the Infinity Engines. "May I take a look?" Dad carefully opened a case to show Quinn the complex cube.

"Remarkable," he said. "I imagine it would make a big difference if we had enough of them."

Dad nodded. "Clean energy for vehicles could help slow down global warming. Affordable energy would make a big difference for folks everywhere."

Quinn looked at Dad. "Can you can make more of them?"

"We know how to make them, but it would take a lot of help to build enough to make a difference," Dad replied. "Our labs aren't designed for mass production."

Quinn turned to his aide. "Don't we have something called a Department of Energy?"

She smiled. "Yes, Mr. President. That would be a great place to start. I can put them in touch with the secretary of energy right away."

Quinn smiled and looked at Mom and Dad. "How would you like to work with them? You could lead our new Clean Energy program."

Mom looked concerned. "Only if we can control how it is used." She looked over at the soldiers and Pants in the cage. "Only for peaceful purposes. No weapons. And we want to share the technology with the world."

Dad looked up at Meow and SLAYAR and nodded toward them. "We'll need to share with more than just the world," he said.

"You're right," Quinn said. "It seems we have some promises to keep and some hostile fleets to calm. Let's get them out so we can talk. If we can give an Infinity Engine to both sides, maybe we can help them toward a productive peace."

He paused.

"I am concerned about our friends using this responsibly. Do you think we can trust them to behave?"

Javi thought about the fleas and smiled. "We've got that covered, Mr. President. No problem."

# 38

## Phewph, We Did It. Again.

**M**ax and Min searched with Javi for the controls to release SLAYAR and Meow. Min was looking at one of the control panels nearby, when she smelled something awful. "Ew, Max!" She slugged her brother. "That's so gross!"

Max looked hurt and plugged his nose. "It wasn't me, I swear!"

Javi heard the twins arguing and walked over to see what was wrong. "Whoa!" Javi winced. "That is not good. Hold on, what's this?"

Javi noticed some movement under a table and

bent down to look. "Is this Huggs's dog?" Javi sat down and coaxed the frightened pug out and onto their lap. "You're the little stinker, aren't you? Aww, did you get left behind?"

Max, recovering from the smell, knelt down to give the dog a pet. "He's cute!" He looked at the bone pendant around his neck. It was heavy and smooth but had no identification.

Max looked at the collar and saw a name embossed in the leather. "Dig Doug? Is that you?" The dog looked up, panting, a little scared. "What are we going to do with this guy?"

Min looked down and folded her arms. "We are NOT adopting any more animals," she said, a little louder than she needed to.

President Quinn heard Min and looked over. His eyes widened when he saw the dog, and he hurried over for a closer look. "Adorable! You remind me of my favorite pet as a child. Pants convinced me it was undignified to have a pet in the White House, but it gets lonely in there in the evenings."

He frowned toward the cage. "I'm done taking his advice," Quinn said, and squatted down to give the dog a scratch behind the ears. "What do you say, little friend? Doug, is it? Would you like to live in a big, fancy white house?"

The dog lifted his head to lick Quinn's cheek. "I'll take that as a yes."

"I think I found it!" Portillo yelled from across the hangar. She stood in front of a set of controls. "Looks like this is how we can let them out. Are we ready?"

Javi jumped up, excited. "Yes! I've been thinking about how to handle this. I think I can deal with these two. We should release Meow first. He's the more sensible of the two."

Portillo looked back at Quinn, but he was busy handing over his new pet pug to a Secret Service agent for a potty break. "Sounds good to me. I doubt Clown University covered intergalactic diplomacy, so you're the closest we have to an expert."

She pushed a button and the door to the glass chamber swung open with a hiss.

Meow and Pounce wove through the specimens in the chamber and cautiously sniffed around the door before emerging.

Meow walked ahead confidently.

"Does he look different to you?" Max asked Javi.

It was true. Meow moved with a stronger stride.

"Yeah, actually," Javi said. Something had changed.

Meow stepped toward Javi and Portillo and sat upright, Pounce at his side. Javi gave a respectful bow and presented a hand for Meow to sniff. "Chairman, I must beg your pardon for your temporary detention. I assure you it was not our intention, and those responsible will be punished." Javi winked.

Meow gave Javi's hand a ceremonial sniff. "I should hope so. Never have I been treated so rudely. However"—Meow sat up proudly—"I had time to think in there," he said. "I looked closely at the fine feline specimens assembled, and realized that none of them, even the one that so resembled me as a young Feline, felt right."

He looked down and paused to groom himself. "None of them actually were *me*."

"In fact," he continued, "I'm not sure I want to go beyond my ninth life, if it means I have to turn into something different than my own glorious self." He was referring to his aging but still impressive body.

Chairman Meow was a proud Feline, to the very end, and it was his pride that mattered most. "I am irreplaceable," he said. "A new body just wouldn't feel right. If that means I can't live forever, so be it."

"Well said, my friend." Javi smiled.

Meow continued. "We will accept the gift of the Infinity Engine and use it for the good of all Felinus. We can use it to warm up the Arctic Felines in the far north. It can power a new generation of toys to keep our kittens occupied and in top condition. And"—Meow paused to glance at SLAYAR's glaring face, still under glass—"as long as the Binars agree to stick to their own territory, we can agree to be more careful about staying out of theirs."

Javi gave another slight bow. "Thank you, Chairman."

President Quinn approached the group but didn't interrupt.

Javi turned to look at the twins and smiled, one eyebrow raised. "I am so good it's scary," they said, and the twins gave a simultaneous thumbs-up in return.

"Ready for the real challenge?" Portillo said, glancing back at Javi, and then Quinn.

"Work your magic," Quinn said to Javi, who beamed and gave Portillo a nod. She flipped a second switch, and the cube holding SLAYAR and Beeps raised back up into the rafters.

SLAYAR steamed down, furious, Beeps struggling to keep up. "What is the meaning of this? Why was this four-legged freak released before me? I demand satisfaction!"

Javi stepped up. "If I could, I'd like to explain."

SLAYAR skidded to a stop right in front of Javi. "Make it fast, fleshie, because I'm about to get back on my ship and order my fleet to pulverize this place."

"Our deepest apologies, Supreme Leader." Javi gave an exaggerated bow. "We had a temporary lapse of leadership here, but we have things under control as you can see." Javi gestured toward the cage holding Pants and the soldiers. "But we want to make things right."

SLAYAR inched even closer, volume rising. "I was promised the Infinity Engine, and that thing"—pointing toward Meow—"as a prisoner. "Give me both, now!"

"The engine you can have, but not the chairman." Javi raised a hand before SLAYAR could erupt again. "We're done pretending, Supreme Leader. Pants has been put away. It's all over now. We just need to agree on what happens next."

"What happens next," SLAYAR said, "is I get my Infinity Engine. And my fleet. And my dignity, hopefully."

"We all agree with that," Javi said, "but you only get the engine if you agree to a peace treaty with the Felines. They will take the other engine and have agreed in exchange to respect the borders of the Binar territory.

"Meow has promised to stay out of your territory and stop annoying you. No more unwanted randomness, careless chaos. You get your Infinity Engine, and a Feline-free federation. You can return a hero. With the engine, your civilization will flourish, enjoy boundless energy, free of unwelcome interference. All you have to do is promise to use the engine peacefully."

SLAYAR looked at the group and rolled over to examine the engine.

He then turned back to look at the stage, and the guitar he left behind.

A long pause followed.

Beeps rolled toward SLAYAR to check that his power supply hadn't failed.

SLAYAR spun around and rolled back to Javi. "You know what? Fine."

"Really?" Javi didn't expect SLAYAR to agree so quickly.

"Really. Of course, the furry four-leggers are insufferable. Felines are a menace and threat to an organized universe. No respect for mottos and rules. However, if it's true that they will no longer meddle in our metal, I suppose I don't care what they do. I can keep order without destroying everything else.

"And to be honest," SLAYAR continued, "I've been considering a change myself. In fact, I might even like to stay here on Earth for a while."

All eyebrows raised at this comment. Nobody expected that answer, but it soon made sense as SLAYAR pointed at the stage.

"The problem with strict discipline and iron-clad order is that it is so predictable. Am I right, Beeps?"

Beeps sputtered, eye flickering, but couldn't find an answer, so SLAYAR continued. . . .

"Binar is so BORING! I just want to ROCK! You humans have a lot of problems, but your music is out of this world!"

Javi looked at Max and Min and they shared an eye roll. "Good one, SLAYAR."

# 39

## New Directions

**S**LAYAR and Meow came together, snout-to-screen, for the first time. Meow sniffed proudly. SLAYAR's eyes narrowed. "Can we really do this?"

"I know I can," Meow said. "I've had eight successful lives. I accept that mortality is what gives value to life. I'm strong enough to spend my life treasuring what I care about rather than running away from death."

"Uh-huh," SLAYAR said, distracted. He was already bored of Meow's speech. "I just want to rock. It's much more fun than making war plans and chasing after you crazy cats."

Meow shrugged and turned to his faithful number two. "Pounce, you stay here and make the necessary arrangements. I know I can trust you."

"Oh." SLAYAR heard Meow's order and realized he didn't want to deal with any of the details either. "Beeps! I need you to do, um, everything. Got it? Get the engine, make sure nobody tricks us again, you know, all the things. I'm going to be busy."

Meow looked into the light streaming through the hangar doors. "I suppose this is farewell, fleshies," he said, winking at SLAYAR.

"Hey, that's our insult!" SLAYAR shot back grumpily, and rolled back onstage, alone, to take another look at the guitar.

Quinn watched SLAYAR and whispered something to his aide, who smiled and stepped away to make a call.

Meow turned to Pounce. "I am going to return to Felinus now. I'd like to take one more crack at capturing that light, and then I think I'll take part of the fleet out and explore. Chase some comet tails. I'll go as far as I can, while I can."

Pounce agreed. "Never give up, Chairman, that's what I say."

Meow started slowly toward the ship, then turned back. "You know, I rather enjoyed this excursion," he told Pounce. "It was surprisingly invigorating, made me feel like, oh, a sixth or seventh lifer again!"

Pounce smiled and nodded. "You do have a new spring in your step, Chairman. Safe travels." Meow turned and walked gracefully out of the hangar toward his ship.

Pounce returned inside and looked warily at Beeps, who stared back cautiously. "We've been enemies a long time, I'm still not sure I can trust you," Beeps said.

Pounce raised an eyebrow, arched his back, resisting the instinctive urge to hiss at the Binar.

Before they could start an argument, Javi stepped between them. "Peace at last! Come on, you two, let's go take a look at these engines and figure out your future."

Javi led the two over to talk to Mom and Dad.

A bustle of activity followed, Quinn conferred with Portillo, and Mom and Dad reviewed Infinity Engine schematics and designs with Pounce and Beeps.

Max found Obi and gave him ritual scratches. Min checked out Elmer and made sure Pants didn't do any permanent damage.

All the usual noise, the usual things they had missed about each other.

<< The great purr of life, >> Obi thought. << I have missed it so. >>

The sun dropped toward the horizon, when the sound of a landing private jet rumbled through the hangar.

Quinn's aide ran out, excited, and returned with the lead singer of the HEDBANGRZ, a mess of hair and torn jeans, the rest of the band close behind. "Nice venue," she said, taking in the hangar. "Very Area 51."

SLAYAR practically jumped when he noticed the HEDBANGRZ arrive.

"Ajpoiesjf09. Wj3fq0pw93jf!!!"

SLAYAR spit out gibberish, speech circuits overloaded. He grabbed the guitar from the stage and sped down at blinding speed, skidding to a stop in front of the band, still incapable of making sensible sound.

"Oioasjf3290321tftjhgj33 . . ." he blurted out, holding the guitar.

The lead singer smiled. "Sweet guitar." She noticed the flame decals curling up SLAYAR's sides and nodded. "Nice tats, bro. Very metal," she said. She gave a sly look at Quinn's aide, then asked SLAYAR, "Hey, wanna jam?"

SLAYAR, still speechless, filled his screen with a shower of hearts.

"He's kinda cute," she said to the drummer, and SLAYAR started spinning in place, finally speeding back to the stage.

Quinn watched Javi work with Pounce and Beeps setting up peace plans and negotiating a truce.

During a break, he got their attention. "Javi, is it? I'm

quite impressed by your diplomatic skills."

"Really? Thank you! I plan on being a judge one day," Javi said. "When I finish law school, of course."

"You'll make a great one." Quinn smiled. "How would you like to be the ambassador to Felinus and Binar? You don't need to live there, obviously; you seem to know more about them than anyone else on Earth, and I could use some help."

Javi was thrilled. "It would be an honor. I do want to keep taking classes, if that's all right, but I can work with the Wengrods to supervise the transfer of the Infinity Engines to both worlds. I would also like to organize a technology exchange so we can learn from the Binars and Felines. If we could learn to build ships like that"— Javi gestured at the ships outside—"it could be the start of humans exploring the galaxy!"

"Wonderful idea," Quinn said. "I'll let you get started, then." He bowed and let Javi get back to work.

Quinn looked around and searched for Max and Min. He found them outside under the canopy. "Max and Min, I presume? I have a question for each of you, if you have a moment."

They looked at each other, wide-eyed. "Yes, sir, Mr. President!"

Quinn chuckled. "Max, would you agree to be Earth's honorary ambassador to Felinus?"

"Umm . . ." Max was a bit starstruck and stood there, speechless.

"Blink once for yes," Quinn said with a smile.

Max nodded yes, slowly, not sure exactly what he was agreeing to.

"Excellent! And, Min," Quinn continued, "would you be Earth's honorary ambassador to Binar?"

"Uh, yeah!" Min said, reaching out to shake Quinn's hand. "I would be honored." She stroked her chin. "I wonder if I can arrange a field trip for my robotics club. . . ."

\* 🕸 \*

Later that day, after the Felines and Binars had departed with their engines and pride intact, President Quinn returned to the White House and made a surprise broadcast to the nation and the world.

Sitting in the Oval Office, his new pet pug, Dig Doug, on his lap, Quinn told the world about the incredible discoveries, the existence of Felinus, Binar, and the new hope for a better, cleaner future for Earth.

"Today is the beginning of a new era for Humans, together with our new allies, the Felines and Binars. We are not alone in the universe. Our Binar and Feline friends have shown that cooperation is possible, even between groups that are as opposite as you could possibly imagine.

"As for the inventors of the Infinity Engine, they have shown a spirit of brilliance, innovation, and generosity. A wonderful example of the desire to share rather than greedily hoard what they create.

"The future glows bright, my friends." Quinn smiled, happily scratching the dog in his lap. "Keep smiling, and we'll be there before you know it."

The camera shut down, and the broadcast ended.

"Not bad, wouldn't you say?" Quinn said to the dog on his lap, scratching behind his ears. The bone-shaped pendant dangled as the dog stretched his neck for the scratches. . . .

*PFFFFFFFFFFFFT.*

This last butt bomb was neither silent nor deadly but still sent everyone scrambling for un-pug-poisoned airspace.

In the bright lights of the Oval Office, nobody noticed when the dog's collar started to glow.

＊ ◈ ＊

Light-years away, in deep space, a ship drifted, silent and dark. Suddenly, a light appeared, then another—the lights continued to spark in a glittering chain reaction until the outline of the ship became clear in the cold vacuum.

Out of the darkness, an outline emerged, in the shape of an enormous bone.

Inside the ship, a message flashed repeatedly on a small screen, as the ship slowly came to life. . . .

*Who's a Good Boy?*

# ACKNOWLEDGMENTS

The authors and illustrator would like to once again thank all the animals who do such good work caring for our friends, aka their "owners" (what a funny name that is, for such an important relationship!) including:

Simon (Hyde Park)

Gizmo (Omaha)

Mauser (Seattle)

Sophie (Kirkland)

and of course, we'd also like to thank all of *your* own wonderful animal family members!

_____

**(ADD YOUR PET'S NAME HERE)**

_____

**(AND HERE)**

_____

**(AND HERE)**

Give them a squeeze and a scratch-scratch from us!

XO Margie and Lewis (and Kay!)